BLACKOUT IN THE BLITZ

Scholastic Children's Books,
Euston House, 24 Eversholt Street,
London, NW1 1DB, UK

A division of Scholastic Ltd
London ~ New York ~ Toronto ~ Sydney ~ Auckland
Mexico City ~ New Delhi ~ Hong Kong

Published in the UK by Scholastic Ltd, 2009

Text copyright © Terry Deary, 2009
Illustrations © Martin Brown, 2009

ISBN 978 1407 10830 8

Printed and bound by Bookmarque Ltd, Croydon, Surrey

2 4 6 8 10 9 7 5 3 1

GORY STORIES

BLACKOUT
IN THE
BLITZ

TERRY DEARY

ILLUSTRATED BY
MARTIN BROWN

IT'S THE ABSOLUTE BLITZ...

INTRODUCTION

How brave are you?

Do you stand up and face danger? Do you fight against your enemies till you win … or until they smash you like a soft-boiled egg?

Or do you run away?

There are times when running away from danger is a good idea. A very good idea.

Picture yourself on a picnic. You have a bottle of pop, a cake and a plate of trifle. Suddenly a lion appears from the trees and looks at you … it is a hungry lion and it is looking at you and licking its lips…

What do you mean, where has the lion come from? It has escaped from the local wildlife park. It was fed up with just lion around doing nothing, so it popped out for a snack.

What would a brave person do? Attack it with their plate of trifle? No.

Shake the pop bottle till it fizzes and spray the lion in the face? No.

Offer it a piece of cake and hope it would rather eat the cake than your left leg? No.

Those are the things a stupid person would do. A brave person would run and try to climb up the nearest tree.

Now, suppose aeroplanes are flying over your house and dropping huge bombs. They will go clean through your roof, land on your tea table and explode with a blast of heat that will make you into mincemeat. Do you attack the bomb with your plate of trifle? Spray it with pop? Offer it a piece of cake? No.

But bomb attacks are what happened seventy years ago. In the savage Second World War aeroplanes flew over houses, dropped bombs and massacred millions. The bombs didn't mind if the victims were young and harmless like you. The sensible young people hid underground in shelters with their families.

But the really sensible ones ran off to a quiet place in the country, long before the aeroplanes arrived. The bombers were attacking the towns and cities – they aimed for the factories and the shipyards, the railways and the gasworks, the mines and the power stations. But they also aimed to bring terror to the people. They hoped the ordinary people would start crying, 'Stop the war! Surrender!'

The bombers were not bombing the quiet country villages. So sensible parents sent their children off to those quiet country villages and safety.

Tens of thousands of children were sent from their homes. It was called 'evacuation'.

For one child it would be a wonderful new world that they loved and remembered all their lives.

For the next child it would be a nightmare full of horrors.

Which child's story do you think we will follow?

Clue ... this is a Horrible Histories: Gory Stories book.
Dare you read it? How brave are YOU?

BOMBS AND BONES

Sunday 27 October 1940, Coventry

Alf Turner dribbled the shabby, leather football over the cobbles of the back lane and muttered to himself as he ran. 'It's the great Clarrie Bourton racing into the penalty area for Coventry City … he beats one man … he beats three … he raises his right foot … he shoots … and he scores!'

Alf thumped the ball at the black-brick back wall of Mrs Sheldon's yard. It hit a stone and skidded to the left. Instead of hitting the wall it hit the back door. 'It's eight-nil to Coventry City … a new club record!' He cheered … even though he had missed the 'goal' he had chalked on the wall.

To celebrate he banged the ball towards the wall again … and again he hit the green back door. Peeling paint flaked off and there was the sound of wood splintering.

Suddenly the door was torn open and Mrs Sheldon stood there, her faded flowery housecoat wrapped around her and a headscarf tied in her colourless hair. Her face wasn't colourless. It was red with rage. 'What have I told you about banging that blasted ball against my door? Eh? What have I told you?'

Alf picked up his ball and watched her. He put his weight onto his toes, ready to turn and run if she took a step towards him. He didn't answer her so she went on, 'I said I'd go down to your father's shop, get one of his boning knifes and stick it in the blasted ball. Give that ball to me now!' she ranted.

Alf just shook his head slowly. 'Clarrie Bourton wouldn't give the ball to some mad woman,' he said.

Clarrie Bourton was Coventry City's top scorer in the years before the Second World War. He scored 50 goals one season! That is amazing, isn't it? Being a star footballer with a name like Clarrie.

Mrs Sheldon stepped forward. Alf fled. He dodged between the washing that hung on lines across the back street – sheets slapped at him, blouses blew at him and long-legged knickers nudged at him.

At the end of the back lane he turned and looked back. Of course Mrs Sheldon hadn't run after him. He bounced the ball hard on the road then let it soar into the air. He headed it and kept it up while he counted, '… three … four … five…' The ball flew away from him and bobbled across to the corner of the front street.

A girl had been standing there watching him. She picked up the ball, rested it on the palm of her hand and held it towards him. She was as thin as a stick insect. She wore a faded blue school dress even though it was Sunday and not a school day. 'Can I play football with you?' she asked.

Alf blinked. He frowned. He snatched the ball from her and curled his small nose back in a sneer. 'Girls don't play football,' he said. 'You go to my school, don't you?'

She nodded. 'What's left of it. There's hardly anybody left. Even the teachers have gone off to join the army. Mr English is probably shooting guns right now!'

'Tah!' the boy tutted. 'If he's as good as he was firing the blackboard rubber at my head we'll win the war by Christmas. He never missed!' he said, rubbing his rough brown hair at the memory. 'What do they call you?' he asked.

'Sally,' she replied. 'Sally Midwell. So can I play football?'

Alf looked up at the cold, clear sky – clear except for some white vapour trails from aircraft. British aircraft, he was sure. The Nazi's air force, the Luftwaffe, only came at night. 'Girls don't play football, I said.'

She shrugged her bony shoulders. 'You haven't any boys you can play with,' she said.

Alf placed the ball on the pavement and sat on it. 'I know! They've all been sent off into the countryside. So a bomb doesn't fall on their poor little heads. It would blow the nits out if it did,' he spat.

'The Nazis bombed a hospital in Greyfriars Lane –

killed eight women!' she said. 'Mum says it'll be our house next.'

'So why doesn't she send you away – evacuate you with the rest of your little friends?' he asked.

'She says I'm delicate … if I went into the countryside all that fresh air might kill me!'

'Eh?' Alf laughed. 'Fresh air? Kill you?'

'My mam says there's germs in all them animals out there. Cows and sheeps and pigs … filthy, she says. I've never seen cows or sheeps or pigs and that's why I'm still alive. Have you ever seen any?'

'Of course!' the boy sighed. 'Me dad's got the butcher's shop on the corner of East Street and Payne's Lane – next to the Bunch of Flowers.'

'What bunch of flowers?'

'The pub – the pub's called the Bunch of Flowers!' he said and sighed. 'Girls are daft.'

'Do you cut the animals up?' Sally asked.

'Aye. Skin them, chop them, pare the meat off the bones, mince the meat and make the sausages. I help me dad every night after school and I deliver the meat to customers on a Saturday. I've seen more blood than you've seen tea, and more bones than Bedworth Cemetery,' he said. 'And I've never caught no germs from them neither. Me dad needs me to help in the shop – all those ration books to sort out gives him a right headache – so that's why he didn't want me evacuated to … where is it most of them went?'

'Lincoln,' Sally said.

'Lincoln. Aye. Dad says I'm more use here and if a

11

bomb kills me he'll be able to sell me bits in the shop!'

Sally gasped and clutched her throat. 'That's horrible! He wouldn't do that! Not to his own son! I wouldn't want to eat you anyway!'

'Awwww! Girls!' Alf wailed. 'That is a joke! A joke. Girls don't get jokes do they?'

This is not true. Girls DO get jokes, as you know. It's just that girls get different sorts of jokes. Boys like simple jokes ... some girls say it's because boys ARE simple!

'It's not a very nice sort of joke, is it?'

'Me dad's not a very nice man,' the boy said darkly.

Sally nodded. 'Maybe. So can I play football?'

'Aw, man! Stop going on!' Alf cried and jumped up. He picked up a stone and used it to scrawl a goal against the gable end of the row of houses. 'That's the goal, right? You stand there and I kick the ball into the goal. You have to stop me. I get five shots and see how many I score, right?'

'Then it's my turn to shoot?'

'If you're not splattered against the wall so flat we could sell you in the shop,' he muttered under his breath. He counted ten paces away from the wall and scratched a spot in the middle of the road.

'Mind you don't get run over!' the girl whimpered.

'It's not just meat that's on ration, you know,' he said patiently. 'You can't get petrol either ... or if you can you

12

don't waste it driving round the streets running over kids. When did you last see a car in these streets? Now. Are you ready?'

Alf stepped back. He shuffled his feet. He looked at the ball, the goal, then back at the ball. 'And Clarrie Bourton steps up to take this penalty. If he scores then Coventry have won the Birmingham Senior Cup. He steps back … the crowd holds its breath … he shoots and…'

Alf hit the ball as hard as he could. He hit it so hard it hurt his foot even though he was wearing boots. Sally didn't see it. She felt the whisper of the wind as it went past her ear, heard the smack as it hit the wall and then the sting as it whipped her ear on the way back. Her mouth fell open. No sound came out.

'And Clarrie Bourton hit the bar,' Alf muttered. 'But the goalkeeper moved before the ball was kicked so the penalty will have to be retaken…' He looked up at the open-mouthed girl. 'Ready? Don't move this time.'

At last she found her voice. 'Don't move? You could have killed me!' she squawked.

The boy shrugged. 'I told you girls can't play football.'

Her pale, thin face blushed red. 'You're just a bully, you are. You just want to hurt me with that hard ball. That's not playing football proper.'

He laughed spitefully. 'I didn't ask you to play.'

Sally was breathing hard now. 'I hope a car comes along and runs you over...'

'I told you there are no...'

'A police car ... or a doctor's car ... they still get to drive. Or I hope a bomb drops on your head and your dad gets to sell you in his butcher's shop. And I'll tell you what ... I'll be first in the queue to buy a bit of you!'

'Well, I hope you have plenty coupons left in your ration book,' he smiled.

'I'll save them up special,' she said. She turned and walked down the road and turned the corner into her street. Her blue dress whipped at her bony knees then her knees turned watery. 'Ooooh! I've never spoken to a boy like that before,' she shivered. 'Mam says you have to be polite to everybody ... specially if a boy speaks to you. Eeeeh! I don't know what came over me! It's like my mam always says ... don't get your bowels in an uproar.' She clutched her belly. 'I think I just did!'

The girl wobbled her way towards the whitewashed doorstep and stepped over it so she didn't mark it with a dusty shoe. Mrs Midwell was very proud of that doorstep – and the brass letter-box and door handle she kept polished 'bright as the buttons on your dad's uniform,' she always said.

Mrs Midwell sat at the table in the kitchen with two

mugs of tea in front of her. Across the table sat the last person Sally expected to see in her house … and on a Sunday too. Sally's mother looked up with a worried look. 'Sally … your teacher Miss Street's here to see us.'

'Hello, Sally,' the young teacher said brightly. She was wearing her Sunday-black suit and a white blouse. Sally could smell that perfume she always wore in the classroom.

'What's wrong, Miss?'

'Nothing to worry about. But the school has so few pupils, and it's so near the railway yards the Nazis want to bomb, they've decided to close it.'

'Where will I go?'

Miss Street glanced at Mrs Midwell. Mrs Midwell looked down at the red-and-white tablecloth. 'We've decided it's best if you are evacuated.'

'You want to send me to Lincoln … and the germy cows and sheeps and pigs!' the girl cried.

'No. There's no more room in Lincoln. You'll be sent off to Wales.'

'In a ship? You're sending me over the sea?' Sally cried.

Miss Street laughed. 'Oh, dear, my geography lessons haven't done you much good, have they? Wales is just to the west … probably a touch closer than Lincoln.'

'The germs!'

'The fresh air will do you good,' the teacher said. 'You are far too pale.'

'Mum says fresh air will kill me!'

Mrs Midwell looked out of the kitchen window.

'Not as quickly as the bombs,' Miss Street said. 'Your mother will help you pack your bags. You leave on the train next Monday.' The teacher stood up and smiled down at Sally. 'You're not alone, Sally. Be brave. It's for the best. You'll have a wonderful time.'

Something in Sally's mind told her, 'She would say that.' But Sally didn't say it aloud. Instead she nodded and the nod sent the tears on her cheeks splashing on the kitchen floor.

'I'll have a wonderful time,' she muttered.

Of course she wouldn't. But none of us can really see into the future. If we could we wouldn't do half the things we do. I mean, I wouldn't walk out in front of that bus and get flattened next Thursday! Hah! Only joking. Sorry, it's another boy joke.

16

Sirens and songs

Alf dribbled the ball through the streets and past a pile of sandbags. House owners could use them to shield their doors from bomb blasts.

Not many people had used them … it meant climbing over a sandbag wall when they wanted to go in and out of the house. So they'd turned damp and started to rot where dogs had widdled against them.

They smelled nearly as bad as the bins on the street corners where people put their scraps of food to feed the pigs. The bins were emptied once a week but in summer you could see the clouds of flies a mile away.

Alf jumped off the road as a tram clattered past, sparking on the overhead electric cables and screeching like chalk on a damp blackboard.

There were white lines down the edges of the pavements to help guide people in the blackout and he tried to keep the ball running along the line as long as he could. He was getting good at it but it wasn't the same as having the lads to play with. He wondered if they had trams in Lincoln?

It was turning dark when he reached the back lane behind the butcher's shop on East Street. He dribbled the ball around the horse-droppings from the delivery carts and through the double gates at the back of the shop.

'Hi, Dad,' he called. 'Want a hand?'

Mr Turner had the carcass of a pig hanging from its back trotters by hooks. He was chopping it down the middle with a cleaver. He was neat and powerful. The butcher wasn't a tall man but his shoulders were as broad as those of the dead cattle that hung in the large fridge. He was the strongest man Alf had ever known.

'No, son, just getting this pig ready for opening tomorrow. When the street hears we have a new delivery there'll be a queue past the Bunch of Flowers,' he said with a nod to the back of the pub next door.

The smell of the stale dregs of beer in the barrels mixed with the sour smell of the bones stuffed into sacks in their own back yard. Tomorrow, Monday, was the day the bone man came to collect them.

The smell wasn't too bad at this time of year. But in summer the stench of rotting bones and the ooze of maggots could kill a Nazi at twenty paces ... at least that's what Mr Turner said. 'We'll never be attacked by Nazis while we have the bone sacks full!' he'd laugh.

He was lying, of course. Just a little fib. But sometimes parents think it's a good idea to lie to kids. 'You will LOVE this tasty medicine ... open wide!' 'Eat your greens and you'll grow up big and strong.' Right.

Mr Turner lifted half a pig in each hand and carried them into the fridge. He shut the door and dipped his cleaver in a bucket of warm, soapy water, washing his bloody hands at the same time. He dried them on his greasy, navy-striped apron and took out a cigarette. He struck a match to light it. Suddenly a voice called from the back lane, 'Put that light out!'

Mr Turner stared into the gloom until the match burned down to his finger. He dropped it with an angry cry and the cigarette fell into the soapy water. 'See what you made me do?'

Two men stood there. Alf knew one of them, Mr Park, the Air Raid Protection warden in a black helmet with 'ARP' in white letters. A man stood next to him in a khaki uniform and matching helmet with 'LDV' painted on.

'Oh, it's you, Parksy,' Mr Turner said.

'It is against the law to show a light after the hours of darkness,' the ARP warden said.

'Except it isn't dark yet,' the butcher argued, looking up at the twilight sky.

'The hours of darkness are defined as 18:30 hours this evening. It is now two minutes after that. You are breaking the law.' He turned to the LDV man. 'Isn't that right, Mr Lawson?'

'That's right, Mr Park.'

'I was lighting a match. Those Nazi pilots are going to see that from up in the sky, are they?' Mr Turner sneered.

'Matches are lights. I could have you arrested and fined or even locked in jail!'

Mr Turner picked up a large slicing knife. 'Arrest me? That would be interesting to watch. Pudding-face Parksy. You were a twerp in school and you are still a twerp now,' he said.

Now it is my turn to lie. Mr Turner did not say 'twerp' exactly. He used a much more rude word. In fact it was so rude I would blush to write it down and I would never, ever say it. Trust me, there are words even ruder than 'twerp' and he used one ... in front of his son! I'm shocked.

Lawson of the LDV stepped forward. He had a rifle in his hand. 'He's going to shoot you, Dad!' Alf cried.

The butcher stepped forward, fearless. 'That's right, Air Raid Parksy, hide behind your little LDV friend. You know what we say LDV stands for?' he asked, placing his nose next to the LDV man's. 'Look ... Duck ... and Vanish! I've more chance of seeing off Nazi storm troopers with my lad's football than you have, sonny Jim.'

The LDV man swallowed hard. 'LDV stands for Lawson doesn't vanish! Can I see your National Identity papers sir?' he asked in a choked voice.

Alf held his breath as he watched a slow smile spread across his father's face. Finally the butcher said, 'No.'

'I have a duty to King George…' Lawson began.

Then a wailing noise split the air. It whooped up and down like a ghost that was trying too hard. Hoo-oo-er, hoo-oo-er, hoo-oo-er…

'Air-raid siren!' Mr Park the ARP warden cried. 'To the shelters! Put that light out! Into your shelters! Bombers on their way! Put that light out!' he said running down the lane and back again, then round in circles and then down the lane and out of sight.

The LDV man lowered his rifle. 'We'll leave it for now,' he said. 'But this is my patch … and I'll have my eye on you!'

'Your eye-patch?' Alf jeered.

The man glared at him before he turned and marched down the cobbled lane to find the air-raid warden. 'I could have shot him,' he grumbled to Mr Park.

'You'd have missed,' the ARP warden sighed. 'Put that light OUT!'

Alf turned to a mound of earth that sat by the path in the back yard. Under it was their Anderson shelter – one they'd paid seven pounds to buy, then sweated long and hard to dig out the year before. Now they ended up in it two or three nights every week. 'Shelter, Dad?'

'Aye, son. I'll get the bag,' his father said and ran up the steps that led to the flat above the shop. He was back a few moments later, clutching a bag with water, biscuits, a pack of cards, candles and matches and Alf's mouth organ. It also had all the important family papers and money.

Alf pushed the curtain aside and peered into the damp dark of the shelter. 'Move out! We're coming in!' he shouted. The words echoed off the curved, steel sheets that made up the walls and roof of the shelter.

There was a scuttering and a squeaking as the mice took the hint and ran to hide.

It was the biscuits, of course. Everyone liked a biscuit with their tea. But they always left crumbs and when the raid was over the mice moved in. They ate the crumbs so I suppose you could say they left the shelters squeaky clean! Yes. Another boy joke. You'll just have to get used to them.

Mr Turner lit a candle and it showed a cramped little room. The steel walls were always damp and rusty. A bench ran along one side – Alf and his father could sit on that. If they were there after midnight it became Alf's bed. On the other side was a bunk bed. His father slept on the top. On the bottom bunk his mother had slept when she'd lived there. When the bombing started she went to Yorkshire to stay with her mother – Alf's Granny Joan. 'It's me nerves,' she'd said as she left.

There had been a bit of a row. She wanted to evacuate Alf with her but Mr Turner refused. 'I can't run the shop

AND deliver meat AND clean up at the end of every day. I need the lad to help. We have the shelter. We'll be safe. But if your blasted nerves can't take it you're better off with the Gorgon.'

The Gorgon was Mr Turner's name for his mother-in-law. The real Gorgon was a Greek monster with snakes for hair that turned men to stone just by looking at them. Mr Turner also made a lot of cruel mother-in-law jokes about her like: I say! I say! I say! Did you know, if you arrange the letters in the words 'mother-in-law' you get the words 'woman Hitler'? Disgraceful. Don't do it.

So it came as a shock when the butcher sat down on the bench-bed next to Alf and said, 'I'm glad we've had this chance to talk, son. This afternoon I had a visit from a teacher from your school. Miss Sweet, was it?'

'Miss Street,' Alf said.

'That'll be her. Anyway, she says they're planning to close the school. It was damaged in last week's bombing and it's not worth repairing. There's so few of you left they may as well close it!'

'Great!' the boy cried. Then he remembered the misery of wandering the streets with no friends to play football with.

'They want to evacuate the last kids in Coventry – they seem to think there's even bigger raids on the way!'

'But you won't let them evacuate me, Dad, will you?'

Mr Turner bent his head to the floor so the candlelight

didn't catch his eyes. 'Now, son … you know I would never want to do that … but…'

'But?'

'But … this Miss Sweet Street said there's no room in Lincoln – they'd be sending you off to Wales … farms in Wales. See?'

'No, Dad.'

Mr Turner stood up and walked the short length of the shelter as he spoke. 'Customers come in the shop. They give me a coupon and I give them the meat – if they have a coupon for four ounces I give them four ounces. Yes?'

'I know that, Dad.'

'No coupons, no meat. BUT…'

'But?'

'If they want meat – and have no coupons – they'll pay anything to get it! They'll pay double … treble!'

'But we can't sell them it without a coupon – you'd go to prison for five years the policeman said when he nearly caught you. He said selling meat without coupons is the black market.'

'Correct. And I was nearly caught because I sold all my supplies but didn't have the coupons to show for them.' The butcher sat down suddenly. 'Now, suppose … just suppose … I had the odd sheep or cow that nobody knows about? I can sell it for a fortune!'

'Where would you get that from, Dad?'

'I'm coming to that … suppose I had a friend on a Welsh farm – a farm so quiet no one would miss the odd sheep or cow … good Welsh Black cattle … very tasty.'

'Me?' Alf said, nodding slowly.

'You get billeted with a farmer...'

'Billeted?'

'That's what they call homes that take in evacuees ... billets. You get a billet on a farm. Offer the farmer two pounds for a sheep ... more than he'd get at market! I carve it up and sell it to customers that've run out of coupons. Poor old people like poor old Mrs Potts? The farmer's happy and the customer's happy ... and you and me have a bit of money too, eh?' he said nudging his son in the ribs. 'Everybody's happy!'

'Except the police.'

'Ah – well, yes ... yes ... no ... they would NOT be happy. But who's going to tell them? You and me? The farmer? The customer? No! We're all breaking the law together, you could say. But no one gets hurt!'

'Except the sheep!' Alf joked.

The air-raid siren was still wailing when a voice came from outside the curtain. 'Coo-ee! Mr Turner? Can I come in your shelter?'

Alf groaned. 'Oh, no! It's that Mrs Spencer from the pub next door!'

'Nice woman,' his father said in a low voice, then called out, 'Come on in before a bomb gets you!'

The curtain was pushed aside and a large woman about his mother's age squeezed in and sat next to the butcher. 'Ooooh! Thanks, Mr Turner.'

'Call me Tommy,' the man said with a grin that looked stupid on his hard face, Alf thought. The woman reeked of stale ale and tobacco smoke from the pub mixed with lashings of cheap perfume and powdery make-up. Not at all like the sweet smell of Miss Street, Alf decided. The woman's lips were scarlet with lipstick and her cheeks rose red. Her dress was white and tight with a pattern of purple and green flowers.

'Ohhhh! Thanks, Mr Turner … Tommy,' she said squeezing close to him. 'The air-raid siren went off and I was all on my own in the pub. I'd have been all alone in that cellar of mine. Creepy!'

The butcher was still grinning as he took her hand in his. 'You're more than welcome here, Mrs Spencer…'

'Ivy.'

'Ivy! Room for a little one!'

The landlady giggled like a girl. Alf felt sick. The two adults chatted away as if Alf wasn't there until his father said, 'Here, Alf, give us a tune on your mouth organ.'

The boy nodded and pulled it from the bag. As he began to play his father suddenly burst into a tuneless song while Ivy Spencer fluttered her long, black lashes and looked on, adoring.

'You made me sigh for, I didn't want to tell you,
I didn't want to tell you,
I want some lovin' that's true,
Yes I do, indeed I do, you know I do,
Give me, give me, give me what I cry for,
You know you got the brand of kisses that I'd die for,
You know you made me love you!'

Alf almost choked on his mouth organ. Watching the couple was like eating treacle. He wished one of Mr Hitler's bombs would fall on the roof of the Anderson shelter.

Yes, his dad was showing him up. YOUR parents show you up. It's what parents do best, showing their children up. You just have to learn to live with it because it never gets any better. Sorry.

'Any chance of a nice lamb chop … off the ration?' Ivy Spencer asked in a coo like a turtledove.

'Me and Alf have plans,' the butcher said, winking at his son. 'You'll soon be eating best fillet steak, mark my words!'

'Ooooh!' the woman cooed.

The boy wondered if 'poor old Mrs Potts' was really the reason behind his Dad's scheme.

Alf felt a trickle of cold run down his spine. At first he thought it was the damp from the inside of the shelter, then he realised it was fear … a fear that there was more than the black market behind his father's plans to send him away … get him out of Coventry. Get him out of the house.

> *'Give me, give me, give me what I cry for,*
> *You know you got the brand of kisses that I'd die for*
> *You know you made me love yooooooooou!'*

CAP AND COMICS

Sunday 3 November 1940

The next Sunday was Alf's last before he was evacuated. He and his Dad ended up in the shelter again with Mrs Spencer.

Alf had pulled the curtain aside and looked up. Searchlights were carving the sky, searching for enemy aircraft but finding only cold clouds. The sirens sounded again, for two minutes on the same note, which meant 'All clear.'

'False alarm,' Mrs Spencer sighed. 'I'll be able to open the pub tonight. Will I see you later for a drink, Tommy?'

'I have to help young Alf pack and then I'll be round,' he promised.

Mr Turner led the way through the back of the shop and up the stairs to the darkened flat. After he'd pulled the blackout curtains across he switched on the weak light bulb. He'd placed the bag on the table and took out a stack of one pound notes, fastened with an elastic band. 'There you go, son, there's twenty pounds there. We'll hide it in the secret pocket in your jacket and you can buy as much meat as you can with that.'

Then he went on to explain the details. How Alf would phone the day before to arrange for his dad to drive over to Wales and collect the carcasses.

'Where will you get the petrol from, Dad?' he asked.

Mr Turner smirked, 'Black market, son. A nice bit of black pudding and tripe for old Murphy in the garage and I'll get five gallons … no questions asked.'

Together they packed Alf's small cardboard suitcase with spare clothes, just like the evacuee book told them. Alf would travel in his school clothes: shirt and pullover, short trousers, grey socks, black boots, blazer and overcoat. He'd wear his school cap too. 'I look stupid in that cap,' he moaned.

'No, son!' Mr Turner cried. 'You can't say that! If you ask me you look just as stupid without it. Heh! Heh!'

Alf glared at his father. He wanted to ask about Mrs Spencer but didn't know what to say. 'What else will I need?' he asked, looking at the list.

'Gas mask,' Mr Turner said. He pulled a cardboard box off the shelf and checked that the black rubber mask was inside.

Alf hated the mask. When they had mask practices in school the little windows steamed up and sweat and spit gathered in the bottom of it. When he blew to clear the mask he made a rude noise.

Now, some of the boys in the class did that on purpose for a laugh. Alf was really, really just doing it to clear the spit … at least that's what he said.

Do you believe him? Yes. But what if I told you the trumpeting sounds came out a bit like 'God save our gracious King'? Then you may just think he was having a bit of fun? His teacher didn't get the joke.

30

But Mr English had slapped him across the back of the head anyway. That was nothing new. When the lads had used their masks to smash at one another like knights, Mr English had smacked the back of his head then too.

Alf's name was on the box and his name was on a label on a piece of string that he'd wear around his neck. They'd all been given one when the evacuations had started back in September last year but Alf's had been shoved in the bottom of his gas-mask box and was a bit shabby now.

Mrs Turner had sewn name tags into every scrap of clothing that Alf wore, even his boots. His dad had explained. 'See, son, if a kid is hit by a bomb they get blown into hundreds of little bits. Now, if there are labels on the clothes they can put the bits back together and give them a nice funeral.'

'Aw, dad!' he'd complained. 'I don't like to think of me being blown into a hundred pieces.'

'Neither do I, son. The cost of funerals these days is shocking. Shocking!'

Mrs Turner had snivelled into her handkerchief and moaned, 'I wish you'd let him come with me to Yorkshire!'

But Alf had stayed and he hadn't even been blown into two pieces. With his dad's help he finished packing the case. 'A bull's eye torch,' the butcher said, slipping it inside the case. 'And two new batteries. A couple of comics to read on the train…'

Alf's favourite was the *Beano* with the wicked ostrich, Big Eggo.

'Can I take my football?' Alf asked.

'No point, son. They play rugby in Wales. Funny people, the Welsh ... but very nice,' he put in quickly. 'You'll love it over there!'

'Good,' Alf said as if someone had just told him they were about to stick a needle in his arm but he wouldn't feel it at all ... something the school nurse had told him the week before. His arm was still sore.

'The train leaves early,' the butcher said. 'So have an early night, we'll have breakfast about five and catch the tram to the station, all right?'

'You going to the Bunch of Flowers?' Alf asked.

'A quick pint ... if there's an air raid get to the shelter pronto and I'll join you. All right? Night, night, sleep tight, mind the fleas don't bite!'

'Night, Dad.'

And Alf went to bed and slept like a well-fed dog.

***

Monday 4 November 1940

A few streets away, Sally Midwell hardly slept at all. At 4 a.m. Mrs Midwell was boiling kettles of water over the fire and filling the tin bath she'd brought in from the yard. At 4:30 a.m. Sally was soaping herself and trying not to cry into the cloudy water.

'Your dad's been on the phone to Ludlow,' Mrs Midwell told her daughter. 'Now it seems there's a vicar and his wife live over the Welsh border in a place called Sant. They're looking to take an evacuee in their vicarage.

That'll be lovely, won't it?'

'Will I have to go to church every Sunday?' Sally muttered.

'Probably … you can say prayers for your mum and dad back here in Coventry, can't you?'

The woman tried to sound cheerful but the words just made tears gush down her daughter's cheeks. She washed them away with a soapy flannel. She knew she had to look brave so her mother could keep up her brave act too.

'I'll pray every night too,' she promised.

'There's my good girl. Now, out you get, dry yourself in front of the fire … you can use my best talcum powder, and by the time you're dressed your breakfast will be ready.'

The breakfast would have made even you cry. 'Scrambled egg on toast,' Mrs Midwell said.

Sally looked at the yellow-grey sludge on the plate. 'Powdered egg?' she asked.

'Yes … yes, but it's made from real eggs. Eat it up, girl … there's a war on you know. You remember the rhyme?' she asked and repeated it…

> *'Auntie threw her ham away,*
> *To the lock-up she was taken.*
> *There she is and there she'll stay,*
> *Till she learns to save her bacon.'*

Sally tried to force the egg down. It was nearly as bad as the whale meat they'd eaten the week before when they ran out of ration coupons for fresh meat. She washed the powdery taste away with a mug of tea (without sugar) and collected her suitcase from the door and her straw school hat.

It was still dark outside as Mrs Midwell took her hand and led her daughter to the corner of the street. A biting wind chilled Sally's legs and she shivered inside the navy overcoat. She could think of nothing to say.

A cheerless poster at the tram stop showed a picture of a dead man in the gutter. The message warned people to be careful in the blackout...

'It wasn't far ... just a few yards across the road. He wanted to catch the bus home, so he took a chance and ran for it. Death happened to get in his way!'

Sally was worried that death would get in her mother's way.

At last the creaking, dark tram arrived and they climbed aboard. 'Two to the station,' Mrs Midwell said to the young woman conductor. The tram ground along the streets. Workers got on to go to the factories – factories that made vehicles to win the war ... and made important targets for the enemy bombers to flatten. Maybe that's why everyone was so quiet.

When they reached the station it was starting to get light. Sally saw a boy in a cap climb off the tram in front of her and groaned. It was that awful Alf Turner boy. She was glad there would be hundreds of other children to lose herself among.

They weren't there yet, she noticed. Her mother clutched a handkerchief to her mouth and chewed on it as she said for the seventeenth time, 'You'll be fine. You'll be happy. You'll not miss your mum and dad at all.'

Sally nodded. The train stood at the platform, hissing and grumbling. A little black tank engine with just three carriages, smelling of smoke and oil. It would be crowded, Sally thought, with hundreds of children in just three carriages. She remembered the pictures in the newspapers from the year before. The platforms were full of children with their cardboard suitcases, gas-mask cases and labels.

'All aboard for Birmingham, Telford, Shrewsbury and Ludlow!' the man cried.

'Where are the other evacuees?' Sally asked him.

'We're only expecting two today ... a girl and a boy. Which one are you? Ho! Ho!'

Sally didn't smile. He opened the carriage door and called across the platform. 'Right, sonny, say goodbye to your dad!'

Alf nodded and said, 'Bye then, Dad.'

'I'll ... erm ... wait for your phone call,' the butcher said in a low voice. 'Have a good journey!'

Then he turned and walked away. Alf felt a sudden panic just like when his mum had gone up north. But he couldn't help noticing his dad was whistling. And the tune was that awful *You know you made me love you*.

'Excuse me sir, but were you thinking of travelling today? Because the driver is running out of coal waiting for you,' the railway guard asked Alf.

Alf knew sarcasm when he heard it. He smiled sweetly at the guard and said, 'After you, Claude!' That was a catchphrase from a radio programme he listened to with his dad.

'No, after you, Cecil,' the guard said.

Last time Alf had said that to Mr English he'd got a smack round the head.

There is a lot of head-smacking going on in this story, isn't there? It was pretty common in those days. Look closely at people who lived through the 1930s, 40s and 50s. The backs of their heads are still flat from the smacking. And if you don't believe me I may have to smack you round the back of the head.

The guard held the carriage door open. As Alf climbed into the carriage the guard smacked him round the head. The door clanged shut behind him. The only person in the compartment was that Sally girl. She hid behind a copy of the girly comic, *Girls' Crystal* and pretended he wasn't there. He thought he should try to get her to chat.

'The locomotive's a Fowler 0-6-0 Tank, number 7165,' he said.

Sally glanced at him as if a Martian with green skin had stepped into her carriage.

Most girls don't understand trainspotting. Most boys don't understand why most girls don't understand trainspotting. So, girls, if you meet a trainspotter just look interested. When he says 'The locomotive's a Fowler 0-6-0 Tank, number 7165,' just nod and say, 'Wow! That is so-o interesting!' And, boys, if you want to impress a girl never EVER mention trains. Got it? Sorry I mentioned it.

'It's going to be a cheerful sort of journey,' the boy said as he threw his suitcase, gas mask and cap on the luggage rack. 'I just hope it's a quick journey.'

Of course it wasn't.

The train shuffled along the track then it stopped at a signal. It stood there, steaming, for no reason at all. Then it shuffled off again. (Fowler 0-6-0 Tanks were never famous for their speed, as I am sure you know.)

Alf finished the *Beano* for the third time and put it on the seat beside him. He took out his mouth organ and started to play. Sally looked up from her comic and glared at him.

He rested the mouth organ on his knee and started to sing the words...

'I'll pray for you while you're away,
Each night and day, I'll pray for you,
I'll pray for you till troubles cease,
Then you and I will live in peace.'

He looked across at the girl. Tears were running down her face. 'What?' he asked.

'Nothing,' she said.

'Want to read the *Beano*?' he asked. 'That'll cheer you up. There's jokes in it … like … I say! I say! Where does Hitler keep his armies?'

'Up his sleevies,' the girl said.

'Uh? You've heard it?' Alf gasped. 'Dad always says girls don't get jokes.'

Sally had to smile. 'Swap? You can read my *Girls' Crystal*,' she offered.

He was about to scoff at the idea, but the truth is he'd always wanted to know what went into those comics. He picked it up. '*Pat on Treasure's trail … the clue in the Mystery Mill.*'

'It's exciting,' Sally said. But Alf wasn't listening. He was already lost in the tale of '*Patricia Mulvaney … a girl* (the comic said) *who was not the sort to be scared by a bull…*'

By the time they reached Telford, Sally was laughing at the tricks of Lord Snooty and his gang. She had forgotten her fears of the country.

But Sally Midwell WAS the sort of girl to be scared by a bull. As she would soon find out…

TRAIN AND TRAP

Monday 4 November 1940, Sant, Wales

'The train is late,' the Reverend Rees said. He marched up and down the bleak platform and looked along the line for the fiftieth time. There were no signs to show which station this was.

This was a cunning plan. Road signs, town names and station names were all taken away. Why? This was the plan ... if an enemy spy landed he would soon be lost. He would wander around in circles and never find the army camps, airfields and factories he was sent to spy on. The trouble is it was Brit people who got lost. Enemy spies had maps and compasses to help them. Well, it seemed like a bright idea at the time.

'I hope there hasn't been an accident.'

His thin nose pointed to the east as if he were sniffing for burning carriages. His watery eyes squinted behind gold-rimmed glasses. His black suit was threadbare but his shoes shone bright as wet coal.

'Sit down, Reverend, and stop fretting,' the woman said. Her nose was thin and swooped down to meet a chin that turned up to meet it. That made her whole face as curved as an axe blade and her lips were sharpest of all.

'I wish you'd call me Charles,' the man muttered.

She ignored his plea. 'Tell me about the telegram,' she ordered.

He took it from his pocket again. 'There are just two children on their way. One is a boy – strong and fit and suited to farm work. The other is a girl. She is timid and polite and her teacher says she behaves very well. Between us I suppose we have to decide which we will billet.'

The woman's colourless hair whipped in the wind from the Welsh hills. 'I don't like boys,' she said. 'They are cheeky, unruly and too hard to tame. I like my workers to be like my sheepdogs,' she said and patted the two black-and-white collies that sat by her side. 'Isn't that right, Meg and Moss?'

The dogs looked up at her, fearful, and didn't even wag one tail.

The vicar frowned and shook his head. 'Ada, I don't think you have quite the right idea…' he began.

'Of course I have. We have a boy on the farm, Tegwyn, to do the hard work. Now he was a real lad when he first came to us. It took us nearly a year to break him. We had to starve him, tie him up, beat him nearly every day! Now, now, he does as he's told! See? Boys are trouble, my Morgan says. Girls are easier to break.'

'But we aren't looking to employ workers!' the vicar said. 'We are here to give them happy homes, far from the terrors of the bombs and the Blitz.'

The woman looked at him as if he had crawled out from the nearest pond. 'I need a girl to help with the women's work. You know I was up at five this morning, feeding the geese and the chickens before I got Morgan's breakfast ready? Now, with a girl, see, I can leave all that to her, can't I?'

'But she has to go to school, Ada!' Reverend Rees said.

'Exactly! You see how perfect that is? She gets up, feeds the animals, has breakfast ready for Morgan and Tegwyn and then she can toddle off to school. She'll be back by half-four and she can help with the evening milking, making supper, cleaning the house and mucking out the plough horses!'

'I must say, Ada, I think that would be working her a little hard. Surely a boy would be stronger?'

The woman scowled till her nose almost met her chin. 'Boys don't do washing, cooking and cleaning. Reverend, you have a soft life down there in the vicarage. If we're stuck with a slum brat we make sure it works for its keep.'

'But you are being paid to look after the child,' Reverend Rees argued. 'Ten shillings every week!'

Ten shillings is what adults call 'old money'. When old money changed to 'new money' that ten shillings became 50p. Today 50p may buy half a cheeseburger. In 1940 it would feed a child for a week. This is something called 'progress'. Don't worry if you don't understand it. Neither do I ... and I am so old I remember old money!

'And we are very grateful for the money too. Me and Morgan deserve a few luxuries.'

'But the money is to pay for her...'

'We get the girl. You get the boy, Reverend. That's the way it is.'

'If you say so, Ada,' the man sighed, defeated.

He retreated into the waiting room and sat by the miserable, smoky fire that the porter had lit. It was afternoon before the train finally appeared in a cloud of steam and soot, pulling up the hill to the station.

The porter waited on the platform. 'Station stop!' he cried. 'Station stop! Everyone out who wants this station!'

Alf slid the window of the carriage down. 'Is this Sant?' he asked.

'Can't tell you that, son. Not allowed. It's against the law!'

'What?' Alf asked in disbelief.

'I mean ... you could be an enemy spy, couldn't you? You could be plotting to plant a flare in the woods tonight and guide the enemy bombers to us!'

'Why would the enemy waste bombs on your woods?' Alf asked.

'Yes ... well ... you could creep into Sant village and plant a flare there!' the porter argued.

'Oh, so this is Sant Station, is it?' Alf smiled and reached out to turn the door handle.

'Yes ... er ... no!' the porter squawked. 'I didn't say that!' he turned to the Reverend Rees and Ada Pritchard. 'You heard me not saying that didn't you?'

'It's all right, my man,' Charles Rees said. 'I think these

are our two evacuees from the city come to stay with us. I have a telegram here from their school. I don't think they are enemy spies.'

The porter stuck his chin up. 'I never thought they were ... but careless talk costs lives ... it says that on the posters, doesn't it? And you never know who may have been listening, do you?'

'A very good point, and the country will be safe in the hands of men like you!' the reverend smiled.

'Thank you, sir. I does my duty.'

'Now,' the vicar said. 'You must be Alf Turner,' he said, peering at the boy's label and picking up his cardboard suitcase. 'I'm the Reverend Rees. You're coming with me.'

Sally stood silent behind him, wanting to speak but too afraid.

'No! I don't think so,' Alf said quickly. 'I have to find a farmer...'

But the vicar was already heading for the door that led through the station to the road.

'Why would you want to live on a farm?' Mrs Pritchard asked sharply.

'My Dad's a butcher ... he sent me to do a deal on cattle and sheep...'

'Hurry along, young Alf,' the vicar said, placing the boy's suitcase carefully on the back seat of a small Austin Seven car.

'What sort of deal?' Mrs Pritchard asked, moving after them and ignoring Sally. The girl was swallowed in smoke as the train pulled away.

'You know…' Alf said. He lowered his voice. 'Black market? I've got cash!'

'Cash?' Mrs Pritchard muttered. 'Maybe you should come with me and we can…'

'Hurry up, Alf!' the vicar called. 'The engine's running and petrol is precious. There's a war on, you know!'

Alf climbed slowly into the passenger seat as the farmer's wife hurried after him. 'I've been thinking about who should have these children, Reverend,' she began.

'So have I!' Charles Rees cried. 'And you are right after all. A strong boy can cut my wood for the winter, fetch coal and dig the vegetable garden over. He can clean the car and tidy the garage … there's years of junk in there. Yes, a splendid idea of yours, Ada!'

He gave two toots on the horn and pulled away. Ada Pritchard looked after him and cried, 'Oh, bums!'

I tell a lie … but only a small one. She said 'Oh, bums' but in Welsh. Now my Welsh isn't very good. She may have said, 'Bum' and been talking about the vicar. That is a very rude thing to say to a man of God. Please don't do it next time you see a vicar at a wedding or it'll be your funeral.

Sally stood and looked at the fearsome woman. She felt sick. She clutched at her *Girls' Crystal* comic. Mrs Pritchard turned to her, furious. She snatched the comic and threw it into a box by the door of the waiting room marked 'Newspapers and Waste for the War Effort'. Her thin lips hardly moved when she spoke. 'You'll not have a lot of time for reading, child. Get in the trap.'

'Trap?' Sally said through the lump in her throat.

'There is a carriage outside – a horse-drawn trap … or were you expecting a motor car like his lordship, the high-and-might Reverend Rees?'

'No … I…'

'Because we don't have luxuries like that on the farm. We don't have electric. We don't have running water. That will be your first job in the morning,' the woman rattled on as she climbed on to the two-wheeled trap and picked up the reins. The dogs scrambled in the back after them. 'Fill buckets from the pump in the yard – if it isn't frozen – and set some to boil so Mr Pritchard can have his shave.'

'And if it's frozen?'

'Then you have to go to the pond with an axe, break the ice and fill buckets from there. Of course the pond is half a mile from the house … but what's half a mile to a young girl like you? It's heavy work carrying buckets up the hill for a woman my age. But you'll do fine.'

The bony horse plodded along the twisting lane with its high hedges. From her seat beside the farmer's wife, Sally thought she could smell the cow-muck on the fields. Then she realised it was the woman's old brown coat that smelled of cows. Sheep cropped lazily on the stony hillsides and crows circled in the dull afternoon sky.

Sally took a deep breath. She had never felt so lonely or lost. But she knew Patricia Mulvaney from *Girls' Crystal* would face the dangers and loneliness without fear. Pat was a girl who was not the sort to be scared by a bull.

'Can I write home tonight?' she asked bravely.

Mrs Pritchard looked at her sharply. 'By the time you've done your evening jobs there won't be time for writing letters. It'll be dark. Maybe tomorrow. But I want to see what you write. I don't want you telling lies to your folk back in the big city, hear me?'

'I don't tell lies,' Sally argued and was surprised at where she found the courage.

'All children tell lies,' the woman spat as she turned the trap into a rutted lane that was not much wider than the wheels. A sign said 'Penlan Farm – No through road – Keep Out. Beware of the dogs.'

Thorn bushes brushed at Sally's sleeve and she shrank away from them. The farmer's wife looked at her and gave a grim laugh. 'Yes, the whole farm is surrounded by thorn hedges ... no way in except this path to the village and another up to the hills. It stops the sheep and cattle straying and it stops thieves getting in.' Her bony hand gripped Sally's arm. 'There's a war on, you know.'

'I know. I've seen the bombs falling,' she said quietly and trembled at the memory.

'Thieves want to take our cattle and sheep. But the thorn hedges stop them getting across the fields ... this lane is guarded by the dogs – they look quiet now but they'd rip your throat out if you make a wrong move. And of course Mr Pritchard has the shotgun. Mr Hitler's storm troopers wouldn't get in here, child.'

'Sleeping beauty's palace,' Sally nodded. 'Surrounded by thorn hedges.'

'Yes. Well even Prince Charming won't get in to set you free!' the woman snorted.

'Free?'

The woman didn't answer. She raised the whip to wave over the hedge to a man as bent and withered and grey-faced as her. 'That's Mr Pritchard,' the woman explained.

'Who's the boy?' Sally asked. A round-shouldered, hollow-cheeked, shrunken young man worked slowly alongside the farmer, pulling up turnips, slicing the green off them and loading them onto a handcart.

'Tegwyn, He's a Gog ... that means he's from North Wales. They're a bit like Trolls – strong as an ox but don't say much and never complain about the work … and when they do it's in Welsh. He sleeps with the cows.'

'Where will I sleep?' Sally asked. 'Not with the cows?'

'No, child. You'll sleep in the hay loft at the top of the barn.'

'The barn?'

'This is a farm, not Sleeping Beauty's palace, even if we do have you shut inside,' Mrs Pritchard said sourly. 'I've heard the stories about you evacuees – half of you wet your beds! Well I'm not mopping up after the likes of you. Of course they pay an extra three shillings and six pence for bed-wetters, so I'll tell them you are one of them anyway.'

Sally tried to tell her she'd never wet the bed but the woman was going on, 'We don't have no fancy guest rooms. You'll sleep where Mr Pritchard lets you and you'll sleep when Mr Pritchard lets you. And if he hears one word of complaint – just one – you don't get to eat.'

Sally wasn't hungry anyway. She feared she'd never eat again. Mrs Pritchard ordered the girl to climb down and open the five-barred gate across the path. The trap rolled through and the dogs stayed behind to guard it.

Sally closed the gate behind her and shut herself in. She had the horrifying feeling that she would die inside these thorny walls.

STRIPES AND STAMPS

Tuesday 5 November 1940

Alf stood at the entrance to the schoolyard and stared out towards the mountains. The iron gates had been taken away to be made into tanks and ships but he still felt as if he were in a prison.

He looked back into the yard where his new classmates were throwing a rugby ball around and chatting to one another in Welsh. He knew they could speak English because the lessons were in English. But they wanted to keep him out.

Then he saw Sally sitting on the ground with her back to a drainpipe. Her head rested on her knees. Alf walked over to her. 'All right?'

She looked up with dull eyes. 'It's awful,' she whispered.

He sat next to her.

His own morning had been hard enough but his was full of schemes to rustle sheep and meet up with his Dad. A week of work wouldn't kill him. But Sally looked half dead already. 'You don't like it then?' he asked stupidly.

She turned her weary eyes on him. 'I sleep in the barn. It's warm enough if I bury myself in the straw ... but it's alive ... fleas, mice and I don't know what.' She shuddered at the memory. 'Mrs Pritchard woke me at five. I had to help her feed the chickens then she showed me how to milk cows into a bucket ... have you ever smelled a cow? Close up, I mean? I thought I was going to be sick. I have to do it by myself when I get back tonight. And I have to carry water to the kitchen so she can make breakfast.'

'They feed you though,' Alf asked, thinking of his own breakfast where at least he'd had a real egg.

'Farmer Pritchard and his wife have bacon and egg and mushrooms in the dining room. She makes me run from the kitchen with it so it's still hot. He tries it. She says if he ever complains it's cold she'll whip me with the stick she uses to drive the cows!'

Alf shook his head. 'Don't believe her. The bruises would show. She'd be in trouble!'

'No. She says if I bruise she'll just tell people I fell over in the barn. Anyway, the farm hand, Tegwyn, has to sit in the kitchen and just gets watery porridge with me,' Sally went on and swallowed tears.

'What does Tegwyn say?' Alf asked.

Sally looked at the boy wildly. 'Say? Nothing! He only speaks Welsh – he's a Gog – and he never even looks at me. I think they treat him worse than they treat me!'

'It's only for a while – till the air raids are over,' Alf said.

The girl shook her head. 'I don't know if I'll last a week. You know what's even worse? The toilets! There's just a shed in a corner of the farmyard … the toilet's just a hole in the ground. They don't have toilet paper – just torn up newspaper. She says I have to clean out the fireplace every morning, chop sticks and fetch coal from the coal shed so it's ready to light in the evening. Then I have to take the old ashes and sprinkle them into the toilet pit to soak up the … the stuff. She says I'll have to empty it at the end of the week! Take a shovel, fill a bucket and scatter it on the fields. I'm sick at the thought. And I can only wash at a freezing water pump outside … no wonder the Pritchards and Tegwyn smell so bad.'

'Write home and tell your mother,' Alf suggested.

'She says she'll read anything I write,' the girl groaned. 'She says the only thing I should write home for is to ask for money – if Mum sends her more money then I'll get fed better.'

'Phone home.'

'Mum and Dad aren't on the phone. We never needed one. We don't run a business like your dad does.'

A whistle went and the children lined up at the entrance to the school – a line of twenty boys and about a dozen girls. 'See you later,' Alf said.

Sally's looked at him wearily. 'Will you?'

'Of course.' Then he said something that shocked even him. 'I'll help you.'

The girl's eyes lit up. 'You will? The wartime spirit? Like Mr Churchill says?'

All stick together against the enemy?'

Alf nodded grimly. 'Except the enemy is this village,' he muttered. 'Mr Churchill also says, "*If you are going through Hell then keep going.*"'

Sally managed a small smile. 'I'll keep going.'

A tall, cane-thin teacher walked over to Alf and slapped him across the ear. 'No talking after the whistle has gone for the end of break.'

'But I didn't know that...' he began to argue. He got another slap.

'You do now,' the teacher said. It was clear to Alf the man never cleaned his teeth. 'And one school rule that even slum children like you must know is, "*Never answer back.*" Am I right?'

'Yes.'

'Yes, sir, Turner. Never forget the "sir" or don't they teach you that in the slums either?'

'No, sir,' the boy muttered and glared at the ground. Mr English, back in Coventry, was hard – and his attacks with the blackboard rubber were harder – but at least he was fair. Alf almost began to miss Mr English.

53

The class trailed into the gloomy classroom and started a maths lesson so simple Alf had finished his sums in half the time of the rest of the class. He stared out of the window at the wintry sky and began to plot. First he had to get some of those black market animals back to his dad. Then he had to try and help Sally get away from the foul farm.

He had no chance to see Sally at lunch. Boys and girls sat in separate rooms. He chewed his way through the awful mess of a sort of stew with mashed potato. Posters grinned down from the walls with cheery messages. A little cartoon potato man called Potato Pete stood by a poem that read...

'There was an old woman who lived in a shoe.
She had so many children she didn't know what to do.
She gave them potatoes instead of some bread,
And the children were happy and very well fed.'

'Bet they didn't eat this muck,' Alf said to himself. Then he remembered the radio programme that had told the listeners how to make 'potato and chocolate pudding'. His Dad's effort tasted more like glue and sawdust pudding.

At afternoon break Alf managed to say to Sally, 'I have an idéa. How about if I write a letter home and tell my Dad to tell your parents what's going on here?'

Sally nodded slowly. 'That might work ... but tell them to be quick. I don't think I can stand this much longer.'

'Leave it to me,' Alf said and was pleased to have found such a simple way out. The last lesson of the afternoon passed more quickly. The class took turns at reading from some ancient copies of an old book about smugglers called Moonfleet. And Alf smiled a secret smile at the thought of smuggling Welsh Black cattle back for the poor people of Coventry. All he had to do was find a chance to talk to the Pritchard woman.

The bell rang for the end of the school day. Some boys raced to the gate so they could trip Alf as he walked through. Alf just stopped. Looked at the boys, one by one, and dared them to start a fight. One by one they let their eyes slide away from his burning glare. He nodded and turned. Alf trudged out through the gates and set off for the half-mile walk to the vicarage and a night of work.

But Sally's work was worse. She climbed the hill to Penlan Farm through the dark tunnel of hedges. The dogs at their gate barked a savage greeting but let her pass. Mr Pritchard heard the noise and ran from the farmyard at the top of the hill with a shotgun clutched in his hand. She knew it would be useless to try to run away through that gate at night.

Farmer Pritchard saw Sally and gripped her shoulder in his bony talon of a hand.

'You're late.'

'Teacher made me tidy the classroom after lessons,' she said.

'Teacher needs to be told your place is here on the farm. Now get in the barn!' the man said.

The Welsh Black cattle stood in rows, tied in their stalls, waiting to be milked. 'Get on with it, put the milk into the churn on the trap and I'll drive it down to the road to be collected,' the man ordered.

Sally began to slow job of milking each cow into a bucket, carrying the bucket to the trap, climbing up the step with the heavy bucket and pouring it into the metal milk churn. It was exhausting and she was hungry.

After an hour Mrs Pritchard came into the yard with a lantern and lifted the churn lid. She peered in. 'Full?' she said in her vinegar voice. 'You get more from the cows that I can, girl!'

'What about the blackout?' Sally cried.

The woman's chin curled up in disgust. 'Blackout? Here in the mountains? Don't be stupid, child.'

'So can I have supper now?' Sally asked.

'Supper? Don't be foolish! Mr Pritchard has another job for you before you can have supper ... and do it right or you won't get to eat at all!' The lantern showed the way back to the barn. There was a bucket of whitewash in the corner of the barn and a brush on a hook.

'There are two cows to go to market on Saturday,' the woman explained. 'The local police say there's a new rule that cows have to be seen on the road at night. We don't want a car crashing into a black cow in the dark, do we?'

'So take them in the daytime,' Sally suggested.

'The market is five miles away. If we are going to get there in time for the opening we have to...' the farmer's wife began. She stopped. She made her hands into fists and waved them around. 'Why am I having to explain myself to a slum girl?' she screamed suddenly. 'Why? Eh? Why? Just do what I tell you. We feed you, give you shelter and I even gave you my old dress to work in so your school uniform stays clean. And what thanks do I get? Eh? You argue with me! Where's my stick? My stick! Where is it when I need it?'

'What do you want me to do?' Sally asked quickly.

'Do? Do? It's obvious. Take that whitewash and paint the cows.'

'Paint the cows?!' Sally gasped.

Yes, I suppose you will be gasping too. What a silly idea, you say. Surely that is too stupid even for a story. No one would paint a cow. It's not ME that's stupid, let me tell you. Because this really DID happen in the Blitz years. Black cows had white stripes painted on them. They must have looked as if someone had dressed them in a football strip.

Mrs Pritchard went into an even greater rage. 'There you go again! Refusing to do what I tell you! There's a war on, you know, and all you can do is give me cheek and question me. Paint the cows. Paint them with white stripes. Do it, just do it – it's the two cows at this end of the stalls. Do it if you ever want to see food again! And don't forget to wash the brush when you've finished.'

She grabbed Sally by the collar and threw her towards the cows, then wiped her hand against her pinafore. 'Urgh! They say you evacuees usually have nits. Well if I find any nits on you I'll duck your head in a bucket of sheep dip. That'll cure you.' The woman turned and walked out of the barn, leaving just a candle to light Sally in her work.

The cows were used to being milked and stood there calmly when Sally did it. But they hated having cold paint slapped on their backs. They raised their feet and stamped and twisted away from the brush. Sally had to dodge their stamping feet and barging bodies. She ended with as much whitewash on the floor and on her legs and arms as she did on the cows. 'Patricia wasn't afraid of a bull,' she told herself. 'But I bet she didn't have to paint one.'

She walked weakly to the bottom of the yard and pulled the pump handle to let the freezing water splash over her. Her hands were numb as she flushed water through the bristles and her feet were like ice blocks.

Her supper was carrot soup with dry bread and weak tea with no sugar.

Sally carried Mr Pritchard's dinner to him from the kitchen. A large cooked bird with potatoes and cabbage. It made the girl's mouth water. Mrs Pritchard nodded at the dish and said proudly, 'There you are, dear ... that crow you shot this morning!'

Sally's mouth stopped watering.

Then, dressed in her woollen nightdress and thin slippers she crossed the yard to her bed in the barn.

She looked down the bat-black lane towards the gate. The eyes of the dogs seemed to glow red and hungry as if to say, 'Try and escape ... just try.'

As she wriggled down into the straw she drifted down into an exhausted sleep with one happy thought. 'Alf is going to write home and tell his dad to tell my parents to rescue me.'

***

Alf folded the letter and placed it in an envelope. He walked down the stairs to the library where Reverend Rees was sitting with a glass of port in front of the large fire that Alf had lit for him. 'Excuse me, sir,' the boy said. 'Could I buy a stamp from you? I can take my letter to the postbox on the way to school.'

The vicar smiled a warm and half-drunken smile.

'Leave it with me, Arthur…'

'Alf, sir. My name's Alf.'

'Yes, yes. Leave the letter with me and I'll make sure it's posted!' he said.

Alf left the letter on the table, nodded and said, 'Goodnight, sir.'

When the door had closed the vicar's smile slid from his red face. He picked up the letter, slid a finger under the flap and opened it. He read it carefully. His mouth turned down sourly. 'Oh, dear, young Alf. This will never do. Oh, dear me, no.'

He reached across the table and dialled.

When the phone was answered he said, 'Ah, Ada? Is that you? Yes? I think there's a little problem you should know about!'

SPITS AND SLAP

Wednesday 6 November 1940

It was almost midnight when Alf's bedroom door opened. The light from the landing cast a beam into the room and lit the sleeping boy.

The man in the black suit stepped up to the bed and stretched out a hand. As soon as he touched Alf's shoulder the boy was awake. 'What is it? Air raid?'

The vicar shook his head, 'You're in Sant, boy, not Coventry.'

Alf rubbed his eyes. 'Oh, yes.'

'Get dressed and come downstairs.'

'Is it morning?' the boy said with a yawn.

'No. We need to go out.'

'Why?'

'It's not for you to ask questions. Just do as you're told. I'll tell you all you need to know when you are ready.'

Alf was downstairs in two minutes. The vicar was wearing an overcoat, scarf and hat. Alf was about to ask, 'Are we going out?' when he remembered he hadn't to ask questions.

The Reverend Rees passed Alf his school overcoat and said, 'Put that box down, boy. You won't need a gas mask.' The man led the way outside and crunched over the frosted gravel to the garage. He backed the small black car out. It glittered in the moonlight thanks to the polishing Alf had given it.

It was a half moon. The people in Coventry called the full moon a bomber's moon ... full moons lit the cities in a way that no blackouts could stop. They learned to fear the full moon.

As the car reversed out, the headlamps swept over the front of the house. 'You haven't got any masks on your headlights!' the boy warned.

'Oh, we don't bother with things like that out here. It's more important to see where we're going. Get in.'

The boy climbed into the passenger seat and the car set off down the drive to the main road. 'Don't the police stop you?'

'The police just make us obey the laws that are sensible,' the vicar replied and pressed his foot down hard. The car wobbled down the narrow road at thirty miles an hour. With high hedges rushing past, it felt faster. The vicar was full of port wine, Alf remembered. He was suddenly glad they were on full headlamps.

Cars in cities drove with headlamps covered up, except for a small slit. Of course the blackout meant that the street lamps were switched off. Drivers couldn't see people on the road. People on the road couldn't see cars. So the cars ran over the people far more often than they did in peacetime. Enemy bombs killed thousands. 'Friendly' cars killed more. Sad but true.

As they drove through the silent village and up the lane into the hills the Reverend Rees said, 'We are going to see

Farmer Pritchard.'

'That's where…'

'Yes, that's where your little girlfriend is staying. Lucky child! Mrs Pritchard is a wonderful woman.'

'But Sally says…'

'How well do you know Sally Midwell?' the vicar asked.

'Hardly at all,' Alf admitted.

'I thought not. I have seen the girl's reports from her last school … it seems she has an unfortunate habit … she tells terrible lies!'

'Does she?'

'Oh, yes! Can't help herself. Why, she would even tell you that Mrs Pritchard is a ruthless, mean and cruel woman when I know she has a heart of gold,' the reverend said with a soft smile. 'Pure gold.'

'My letter…' Alf began.

Reverend Rees patted his coat pocket where the letter lay. 'Don't worry, Arthur, it's safe with me. Let's save ourselves a lot of trouble, shall we?'

Alf just nodded silently. 'But why are we going to the Pritchards?' he asked suddenly.

'It seems that when you were at the station on Monday you said something about buying some cattle?' the vicar explained.

'You're reporting us all to the police for black market trading!' the boy groaned and reached for the door handle. If he had a chance he'd throw himself out of the car and run. He didn't know where he'd go but he had a jacket packed with money. The thorn bushes in the lane were now so near he couldn't even open the door let alone jump out.

'Don't be foolish. I told you the police just use the laws they want and ignore the ones they don't. Constable Howell in the village likes a bit of black-market meat himself from time to time – Morgan Pritchard makes sure he gets it. Don't worry about the police.'

'Then why are we going to the farm?'

'To see what sort of deal we can do, foolish boy!'

'But you're a vicar!' Alf cried.

'And the Bible says our Lord fed five thousand with loaves and fishes. It is my job to see my people are fed ... but I don't do miracles.'

'You do black market instead?' Alf asked.

'A very ugly phrase, black market,' the vicar sighed. 'I like to think of it as helping the needy.'

'That's what Dad says,' Alf agreed. But somehow, when his dad said it, he believed him. The words sounded odd in this vicar's mouth.

The headlights reflected four red dots as they lit the eyes of the sheepdogs at the gate. Their snarling mouths slavered. 'Want me to open the gate?' Alf asked, helpfully.

He was glad when the vicar said, 'No. They'll tear you apart. Let me.' The vicar squeezed out of his door and spoke quietly to the dogs. They wagged their tails and let him pat them. He climbed back in and drove into the farmyard.

Mrs Pritchard stood at the kitchen door, oil-lamp burning in a way that would have had ARP warden Park screaming. They were soon sitting around the kitchen table.

Farmer Pritchard got straight to the point. 'How much are you offering?'

'Two pounds a sheep, five pounds a cow,' Alf said quickly.

'You have the cash?'

'Yes.'

'Where?'

'Hidden.'

'In the vicarage?'

'No.'

'Three pounds a sheep, seven pounds a cow,' the farmer said finally. The narrow eyes of Mrs Pritchard and the narrow eyes of Reverend Rees flicked from one speaker to the other like people watching a tennis match.

'Not worth it,' the boy said. 'We have to find the petrol and the van to come and collect them. That's four shillings and two pence a gallon – two pounds-worth to get here and back in the van. We take all the risks of getting stopped on the road and going to prison. We are paying you twice what you get at market.'

Pritchard glared at him. 'Two sheep for five pounds. Two cows for eleven. Sixteen pounds all in.'

'Fifteen,' Alf said.

The farmer looked away … a sign that he was losing. He looked at Mrs Pritchard. She gave a tiny nod. 'Fifteen,' the farmer said.

'And ten shillings to the church!' Reverend Rees said quickly. 'After all I brought the parties together.'

Alf sighed. 'Fifteen pounds to the Pritchards, ten shillings to the church then.'

'I can have the animals killed and skinned in a week,' Pritchard offered.

'Skinned? You get to keep the sheep fleeces and the cow hides? You can sell them and make more money!' the boy said.

'That's fair,' Pritchard scowled.

'It is,' the vicar agreed.

'It means no one can tell where the animals came from if you get caught at the other end,' Mrs Pritchard said in her sharp voice.

'Dad won't get caught,' Alf said. 'If the reverend lets me use his phone I'll tell Dad to be here a week tonight.'

'Market day. Better make it Thursday,' Mrs Pritchard said. She looked across at the calendar. The night of Thursday 14th November.'

There was a small white circle against the date. Alf shuddered. A bomber's moon.

'Thursday 14th then.'

Farmer Pritchard spat on his hand and held it out. Alf spat on his hand and their spit mingled as they shook hands.

This is an old, but disgusting, custom that still goes on in many places. Wiping your nose on your shirtsleeve is another old, but disgusting, custom that also goes on. But that doesn't mean you should copy it just because you read about it in a book. If you do then make sure you wash your hands afterwards ... not to mention your shirtsleeve.

***

The vicar told Alf to sit in the car. He spoke quickly to Mrs Pritchard. Alf couldn't hear what they were saying. But one person could. Sally had been woken by the car driving into the yard below her hay loft door. She had seen the Reverend Rees and Alf enter the house. 'Ah! He's told the vicar about my terrible life! The vicar's come to rescue me. Oh, thank you, Alf. I'll soon be free.'

Half an hour later she was still watching when they came out of the house. She heard Mrs Pritchard talking to the vicar.

What Sally heard made her gasp with fear. She threw herself into the straw and prayed. 'Please let me die in the night.'

***

The next day, Sally confronted Alf at morning break. 'You showed him the letter!' Sally cried.

'He opened it himself.'

'You should have known.'

'He's a vicar! I didn't think vicars did things like that.'

'This one does,' she said. 'And do you know why?'

'No but I suppose you're going to tell me.'

'Because Mrs Pritchard is his sister … I heard them talking last night after you got back in the car. The vicar told her to be careful because I was a moaner. He told her I'd asked you for help. Then he said he'd take care of things for the sake of her … his sister!'

For a moment Alf was silent. Then he remembered the midnight journey.

'Liar,' he muttered.

'What?'

'You tell lies,' he said.

She pulled up her sleeve and showed the red marks on her wrist. 'Mrs Pritchard dragged me out of bed by the wrists at told me to keep my mouth shut about what goes on up at Penlan. Do you think I made these marks myself?'

'You could have.'

Her eyes burned and she turned to walk away. 'Only one way to find out,' Alf sighed. 'The hard way.'

He waited till Sally had reached the middle of the schoolyard. At that moment the whistle blew for the end of break. As the pupils lined up in silence Alf ran after Sally, grabbed her shoulder, spun her round and shouted, 'You stole my sixpence!'

'What are you talking about?' Sally cried out.

He pushed his hand into Sally's pocket and came out with the small silver coin. 'There. Thief!'

The head teacher, Miss Goodsir, was on duty that morning. A large woman as tall as she was wide … and she was very tall. She couldn't help but see what happened. She marched across the yard and grabbed Alf by the ear. 'To my room. Both of you.'

Sally, still stunned, wandered after them into the gloom of the school. They stood in front of the desk as Alf explained. 'She stole my money,' he said quietly.

Sally's mouth moved, open and shut like a goldfish. At last her voice came. 'I didn't!'

Alf shook his head. 'She is a liar, Miss Goodsir. Everyone knows she was the biggest liar in East Street School. She can't help herself. It will tell you that in her report! Go on! Look at it!'

Sally just shook her head miserably as the head teacher reached into the drawer and pulled out a cardboard folder. She opened it and studied the notes. At last she looked up. 'Quite the opposite, young Turner. She is the most honest child you could wish to meet, it says here.'

Alf gave a wide grin. 'Ah! That's what I wanted to hear, thanks. So the vicar WAS lying.' He looked at Sally and winked. 'Don't worry I'll have you out of there a week tomorrow,' he whispered.

'Sally, you may leave,' the headmistress said.

The two turned to go. 'Not you, Turner. Only a coward and a bully would accuse a poor girl like that. And we know how to deal with cowards and bullies in this school – even if they let you get away with it in your city slum schools.'

'They aren't slums,' he sighed. 'But get on with it.'

The woman reached for one of the canes that stood in a rack behind her desk. She chose the longest and springiest. 'Which hand do you write with?'

'The right hand.'

'Then hold out your left hand,' she ordered.

> You understand that don't you? Maybe you don't, as the cane isn't used these days. So I'll tell you. The torturing teacher asked which hand you wrote with. They then beat the other hand to a stinging, swollen pulp. You could still go back to class and do your written work. See? There is nothing so cunning as a teacher ... unless it's a fox, of course.

A minute later he left the room with a left hand that was burning and red. But he was grinning all the rest of the morning. He even grinned through the corned beef pie and tapioca pudding that was as sticky as glue.

At afternoon break he ran across to the scared Sally. 'It's all right. Sorry I had to do that. But I had to be sure. You'll be out of there in eight days. I'm taking you home under a bomber's moon,' he promised. 'Can you last that long?'

She sniffed back a very small tear. 'Of course I can. Like Mr Churchill says, we never give in. Never, never, never!'

GOD AND GLIDERS

Saturday 9 November 1940

Alf had been hoping for a rest on Saturday but Reverend Rees told him to saw off a branch that had cracked on a tree in the garden. Then he had to cut it into logs for the fire. 'I have to write my sermon for tomorrow,' the vicar explained. 'After lunch I need to visit the men at the hospice.'

'What's that, sir?' Alf asked.

'A place where our brave soldiers, sailors and airmen recover from their wounds. They send them to the peace of the countryside. I bring them comfort for their spirits!'

'I bet they enjoy that,' Alf muttered as he set off to the garage with the saw.

'You can come with me. We leave at one o'clock!' the vicar called after him.

The boy did his work slowly and steadily and let the sawing warm him in the damp, chill air.

It is not easy keeping warm in winter when you have to wear short trousers, of course. But cloth was in short supply in Blitzed Britain, just like everything else. Boys could not have the extra cloth for long trousers till they were 12 years old. So grown-up lads and dads get warm legs – poor weedy little kids get freezing knees. Is that fair?

Squirrels watched from higher in the tree and chattered angrily at him. 'If I had a shotgun you'd make a lovely pie,' he told them. 'Squirrels and hedgehogs – we're supposed to eat you.'

That may sound disgusting but the truth is the man in charge of war food, Lord Wootton, told blitzed Brits they had to look for new types of meat ... such as squirrels and crows – he gave out nice recipes for squirrel-tail soup and bullock-brain broth. And your little fluffy pet bunny would make a tasty rabbit stew. Yummy.

The squirrels glared at him. 'There's a war on, you know,' Alf told them.

Lunch was potato soup and sausage with mashed potato. But there was more bread in the sausage than meat. Alf knew. He made sausages back in the Coventry butcher's shop.

The vicar drove them out onto the road and said cheerfully, 'Your little girlfriend will not get out of Penlan Farm, you know. The place is like a fortress.'

'I know,' Alf said. 'She's a liar, isn't she? It's a lovely place ... we're very lucky to be here.'

The reverend nodded happily and drove on till they came to a large, low sprawl of brick and concrete buildings. A sign said Penglas Hospital. He parked by a glass door and they walked in. The place smelled of antiseptic. Men wandered around in dressing gowns, some in uniforms, others were pushed by nurses in wheelchairs. Some were horribly scarred and one man was almost faceless.

'Heroes,' the vicar muttered. 'Their bodies are shattered but I will build their spirits. I will lead a service in the main hall ... you may wait in the lounge, Arthur...'

'Alf.'

'Alf. Wait in here. Read a magazine or something.'

Alf wandered into the room. The windows were large and looked across lawns to distant mountains. The assortment of armchairs were arranged to look out of the windows. So Alf didn't see that a man was sitting in a high-backed chair till the man spoke. 'Good afternoon,' he said.

Alf gave a small jump. He turned to see a young man with short, dark hair dressed in an air-force uniform. 'I'm with the vicar,' he said.

'Holy Joe? I'm hiding from him and his mealy-mouthed words,' the young man said bitterly. 'Holy Joe tries to tell us God is on our side ... but the Germans tell their people the same thing! *Gott mit uns*, they say ... God is with us. Well if God is with anyone why does he let so many die?'

'I don't know,' Alf muttered.

'Sorry! Sorry!' the pilot cried. 'You don't want to hear me whine about the war and all the friends I've lost. I'm Pilot Officer Ingram ... you can call me Eric.'

'I'm Alf ... from Coventry.'

The pilot nodded. 'A good place to be out of at the moment. I shouldn't tell you this ... but you don't look like a Nazi spy...'

'I'm not!'

'I've been talking on the phone to some of my old mates at a bomber base in Norfolk. They say that last night they raided Munich in Germany ... that's the city where the Nazi party started up. It was a huge raid too.'

On Friday 8 November 1940, the RAF bombed Munich. Hitler said, 'An attack on the capital of the Nazi movement would not go unpunished.' Hitler wanted his revenge. The revenge came quicker than the Brits expected ... as you will see.

'Good,' Alf said. 'Serves them right.'

The pilot shook his head. 'Mr Hitler won't see it that way. He'll see it as a personal attack ... an insult. Trust me, he will order an attack on some British cities as soon as possible.'

'This week ... the bomber's moon,' Alf nodded.

'So you're safer here,' Eric Ingram said.

Alf sighed. 'But ... it's not home. I mean it's hard for some evacuees ... the way they treat us.'

The Pilot Officer just raised an eyebrow, inviting Alf to go on. And Alf did. He poured out the whole story of what had happened since he and Sally had arrived. When he finished he muttered, 'Sorry, it's me that's whining on now!'

The pilot was looking out of the window at the cold skies and thinking. 'I'm here because my Wellington bomber was shot down by ME109s over Berlin ... well, I managed to get her back over France before we had to bail out. But by then the gunners were dead and only me and the navigator got out alive. We were arrested as soon as we landed and taken off to a prisoner of war camp.'

'But you're here now!' Alf said.

'I escaped.'

The boy frowned. Something the vicar had said came back to him. Penlan farm – a fortress ... no escape. 'How did you do it?'

The Pilot Officer took a deep breath. From somewhere in the building men were singing a hymn, *Abide with me*, and it sounded as mournful as a howling dog. He told his tale. 'We pulled up the floorboards in our hut. Then we started to dig a tunnel. We broke the bed posts to prop up the tunnel. We filled our spare socks with the earth and, when we went out on parade, we let the soil spill out onto the ground. The guards never noticed. After 6 weeks we were under the fence and we waited till a moonless night to run for it. Twenty of us got out ... half of them were caught the next day. I heard shots...' The pilot stopped and swallowed hard at the memory. 'To escape we dressed like French workers ... if you are caught in uniform you're a prisoner of war ... prisoners of war have to be cared for. But if you are out of uniform you are treated as a spy. They can shoot you on the spot.'

'That's what happened to your mates?' Alf asked.

'I think so. I was the lucky one. I found a group of French farm workers who set up escape lines – they call themselves the Resistance. They helped me cross the border into Switzerland ... the Swiss aren't in the war. And I was flown home. I still have wounds from being shot down so they sent me here,' he explained patting his leg. 'But I'll be back.'

Alf said, 'That's fantastic ... but...'

The pilot grinned. 'But it doesn't help your friend Sally? I know. She can't dig her way out of her barn, get under the hedges and past the dogs. She doesn't have a team of twenty and she doesn't have six weeks! I know. But I do know there is always a way if you keep trying. Always.'

'Never, never, never give in?' the boy said.

'That's right.'

'So what other ways are there?'

'There are some chaps in here who escaped from other camps by hiding in laundry baskets – the guards just waved laundry vans through the gates.'

'Mrs Pritchard doesn't send laundry out. She gets Sally to wash things in the freezing pump water,' Alf murmured.

'There was another plot where our lads stole tools and cut through the wire fence.'

'Thorn hedges are tougher than wire. It would take all night to make a big enough gap … and the dogs would hear.'

'There were some who copied guards' uniforms and marched through the gates!' the officer laughed. 'I liked that one. I don't suppose you could dress Sally in a sheepskin and see if you can bring her out with the dead animals?'

Alf shook his head. 'The animals will be skinned before we collect them. Farmer Pritchard told me that. Is there nothing else?'

'Show me the layout of the farm – the barn, the fields, the gate and so on.'

Alf took a pencil and some paper from a table and began to sketch what he remembered from his one visit in the midnight hours.

Abide with me had finished and the vicar's voice was droning on with his sermon. The pilot studied the plan for a long while. Then he spoke so quietly Alf could hardly hear him. 'There was one plan we talked about a lot … but we were never able to carry it out. It was crazy anyway. I don't know if it would work. But it's the only way out. If you can't go under and you can't go through then you have to go over.'

'Uh? Sally can't fly!'

'Why not? I did. That's how I ended up here!' Eric Ingram said.

Alf threw his hands in the air. 'So we smuggle a Wellington bomber into Penlan Farm and Sally just flies out. Great idea. Great. Have you got a spare Wellington in the hospital?'

The pilot ignored Alf's sarcasm. 'The farm is on a hill top. The barn has a high roof. You don't need to take off and fly over the gates or the hedges. You just get on the roof of the barn and simply glide over them.'

The boy closed his eyes. 'A parachute? She'd just drop to the ground.'

'No. Look.' Pilot Officer Ingram took a sheet of paper and folded it along its length a few times. He pinched one end then spread the other end out.

'A fan?'

'Or a bat's wing. We make a frame of five ribs and cover it with parachute silk. It's carried to the roof of the barn folded up – very light. Sally just has to spread it out,

hold on to a cross-piece and jump. Instead of dropping –
like you would on a parachute – you soar like a kite. She'll
clear the gate and the dogs and the hedges.'

Alf's mouth was dry with fear at the thought. 'But a
kite has a string. If she sails off what happens if she
doesn't come down again?'

'I've thought of that. You have two very fine, strong
ropes. One is fastened to the back of your van. Paint it
black. In the darkness the farmer will never see it. As the
van sets off it will tow her down towards the road and then
you can wind her in. The second rope just trails underneath
her. If it's a strong wind – and she's flying like a kite – you
can just pull her down to the ground with it.'

The boy stared at the paper fan. 'Will it work?'

'We have some real experts on flight in this hospital. Good
mechanics who've worked with planes for twenty years.

They'd love to make it work. We have workshops and all the materials we need. I reckon we could have this ready in a couple of days … Tuesday 12th.'

Alf nodded. 'Dad could pick it up from here on his way to Penlan Farm. We'd back the truck up to the gate. When they go to fetch the meat I pass the glider up to Sally…'

'Fasten one end to the cab of the van first.'

'I pass the glider up to her … we load the meat and set off with Sally in tow. When we reach the road we haul her down … and take her home. Brilliant!'

'Fool-proof,' the pilot agreed.

'What is fool-proof?' Reverend Rees asked. Alf didn't know how long he'd been standing there. The vicar looked coldly at the boy.

'A paper aeroplane, Vicar,' Eric Ingram said quickly. 'I was showing the boy how to make a paper aeroplane.'

'Oh, dear. You missed my holy service so you could play with paper planes?' Reverend Rees said sternly.

'I missed it because my leg is in bandages and the hospital had no more wheelchairs … but Alf and I listened to the service, didn't we?' He suddenly broke into song. '*A-bide with me-e-e, fast falls the e-ven-tiiide, The darkness deepens; Lord with me abide.*'

'You have a fine voice, Officer,' the vicar said.

'In the Royal Air Force we have favourite line in that hymn,' he went on. He said it strongly but he was looking at Alf. *Shine through the gloom and point me to the skies.*

'Point me to the skies!' the vicar said. 'Yes indeed, my brave chap. Point me to the skies. Remember that fine phrase, young Arthur ... point me to the skies.'

'I'll remember,' Alf said. 'I'll remember.'

***

Monday 11 November 1940

Sally thought about the plan when Alf explained it to her in school on Monday morning. She was thinner and ghostly pale after less sleep and more work. 'If I fall off the parachute-glider I'll probably die.'

'Ah, but you will probably fall around the gateway — Mrs Pritchard will be there ... you'd fall on her head and kill her too!'

Sally smiled for the first time in a week. 'True. I'd like that,' she said. 'I'd like that a lot!'

BEER AND BAT-WING

Tuesday 12 November 1940

'Hello, Dad?' Alf said into the phone. The phone box was near the post office in the village. The boy had plenty of money to feed into the box a penny at a time.

'Hello, son! How's it going?'

'It's all planned for Thursday night. There will be two cows and two sheep, skinned and ready to load. Drive through the village till you come to a lane with a sign that says Penlan Farm.'

'Penlan Farm?' he repeated. Then he muttered, 'Write that down.'

'What?'

'Just asking to Ivy to make a note.'

'Who?'

'Mrs Spencer … the lady that runs the pub.'

'What's she doing there?' Alf asked.

'Helping me round the house, son. Since your mum went away I need a woman round the house. Someone to do the dusting and the washing and ironing,' his father replied.

'Can't you do them yourself?' the boy asked.

'Don't be daft. I don't know one end of an iron from the other! We all have to help one another out. There's a war on, you know. I thought I might bring her on the trip to Wales on Thursday. She can read the map for me.'

'No, Dad. There'll be two of us travelling back with you – there won't be room in the cab if you bring Mrs Spencer.'

'Who's travelling back?'

'Me and someone else. It's a secret, Dad. I've made the contact for you – we can get more sheep and cattle whenever we want. I don't need to stay.'

'Well, I could do with your help in the shop,' his father admitted. 'Who's the someone else?'

'Careless talk costs lives, so I won't tell you who the other person is till you need to know.'

'Spy stuff, is it?'

'Something like that. Now listen carefully, Dad,' Alf said feeding four more pennies into the slot. 'Just before you get to the village there's a hospital on the left. I'll be waiting for you there at ten o'clock.'

'Hospital? I thought you were living at a vicarage?'

'I am. But there's something I need to pick up from the hospital.'

'What?'

'Spy stuff. Top-secret weapon. Nothing for you to worry about, Dad. Just try to time it so you get there as near to ten o'clock as you can. I don't want to be hanging around too long.'

'No, son! The LDV might think you're a spy! If it was that Mr Lawson he'd probably shoot you!'

'There's no LDV here,' Alf explained. 'Just the local policeman. But he heads for the pub at closing time and spends a couple of hours there.'

'You can rely on me, son. I've paid for the petrol with tripe and black pudding. I've got the route marked on the map so I should manage to find you ... and if I set off after I shut the shop I should be with you by ten.'

'Great, Dad, see you then.'

***

Turner put the phone down and turned to Ivy Spencer. 'He's a good lad, Alf. Clever.'

'Takes after his dad then!' the woman giggled as she folded the navy and white-striped butcher's apron and put it on top of the rest of the ironed clothes.

'But it seems he has some sort of plot going on down there. He can't say too much ... but it seems he'll be coming back with me.'

'That makes sense. He's made the contacts. You can go back regular, can't you? The farm probably has a phone. You could be on to a nice little earner there, Tommy. Same as me and my barrels of beer nobody knows about!'

'Speaking of which,' the butcher grinned, 'Pour me another glass, Ivy.'

She poured beer from a jug. 'There you are, Tommy.'

'You're good to me.'

She shrugged. 'You see me all right with steak and kidney – I see you all right with a jug of beer.'

'You scratch my back,' he said.

'And I'll scratch yours,' she smiled. 'That's what the black market's all about isn't it?'

He sipped the beer. 'The thing is, Alf's scheme means bringing someone else back with him. Now the cab of the van is crowded enough with two of us. With four ... well, it would be plain daft to try to squeeze you all in.'

Ivy Spencer sighed. 'I guess that means leaving me behind. Don't you worry about that. I've got the bar to look after. And, tell you what, give me a pound of your best steak and kidney and I'll have a nice pie waiting for you when you get home. You'll be hungry.'

Tommy Turner sighed. 'You'll make someone a lovely wife,' he said.

She sniffed. 'Yes, well you already have a lovely wife so I'd better get back to the pub before it gets dark. We don't want people talking about us!'

She slipped a dark blue coat on and went to the door. She opened it and the cold air struck her painted red cheeks. 'Ooooh! Lovely moon coming up!' she said. 'Very romantic!'

Suddenly a voice called from the back lane, 'Put that light out!'

Mr Turner groaned and turned the light off. 'Good evening, Parksy! What a pleasure it is to see you, as ever!'

The ARP warden had the LDV warden Lawson by his side, as usual. 'See that up there?' he asked pointing over his shoulder.

'Yeah!' Tommy Turner gasped. 'Well I never! Cor, stone me! Look at that, Mrs Spencer. Have you ever seen anything like that?'

'Like what, Mr Turner?'

'Like that chimney pot! Cor, I've never seen such a chimney pot in my whole life.'

ARP Park glared at the couple. 'I was pointing at the moon. That is a bomber's moon,' he said. 'It'll be a full moon on Friday. But that won't stop Mr Hitler sending his bombers over tonight. Isn't that right, Mr Lawson?'

'Right!' the man with the rifle nodded. 'And there will be planes coming over looking for lights like that. They send out a radio signal and the bombers fasten on to it like … like it's a line. A line that pulls them to Coventry.'

'I've got a line. A washing line!' Mrs Spencer said, nudging the butcher.

'Is that the one you hang your knickers on?' he asked.

'Don't be cheeky!' she said and gave him a playful slap on the arm.

ARP Park tried to ignore their teasing and carry on with the warning. 'It just takes one light to give the pathfinders a clue and they'll drop parachute flares. The whole city will be lit up like a birthday cake. There'll be no stopping them then.'

LDV Lawson lowered his rifle and jabbed an angry finger at the butcher. 'See, it's not you that gets hurt. It's the hundreds of other innocent people, isn't it? You show a light and you get blown to bits then it serves you right. But you show a light and some family in the next street gets hammered it's not so fair.'

Mr Turner chewed his lip. 'You're right, Lawson, you're right. Sorry, mate. Here, have a fag.'

He slipped open a packet of cigarettes and gave one to the volunteer. Then he struck a match to light it for him.

'Put that bleeding light out!' ARP warden Park shouted.

'Ooops! So-rreeee!'

***

Alf put the telephone back in its cradle and stepped out of the red telephone box. Mrs Pritchard was coming out of the village store, slipping her ration book into her handbag. The farm hand, Tegwyn, trailed behind her carrying the shopping bags. Her hatchet face was suspicious. 'Everything all right?'

Alf gave her his warmest smile. 'Fine, Mrs Pritchard. Dad will be at your gate between ten and...'

'Hush!' she said quickly and dragged the boy behind the phone box. 'Tegwyn might not speak English but he understands enough of it.'

'Don't you trust him?'

The farmer's wife turned her mouth down till her nose almost met her chin. 'Trust a Gog? I'd rather trust an Englishman! We give him a job, we feed him, we give him half a day off every week, and we even pay him when we've had a good day at market. But is he grateful? No. He hates us! Hates us! If he could do something to spite us he would. We only keep him on because he's the cheapest we can get.'

'So why does he stay with you?' Alf asked.

The woman pulled Alf closer and her sharp voice was matched by her vinegar breath. 'Because he's a conchie.'

Conchie was the slang for 'conscientious objector' – someone who didn't want to kill another person, even in war. Some of these were given dirty or dangerous jobs to do and some were locked in prison. But there were some jobs that were called 'reserved'. That means you didn't have to fight. Farming was one. Lighthouse keepers were 'reserved' – teachers weren't.

'He refuses to fight in the war?'

'Yes, the lily-livered little coward. He can go to prison and do hard labour – or he can do a job to help the War Effort like work on a farm. But come the end of the war Mr Pritchard might just have an accident with his shotgun and blow the conchie's head off his shoulders!'

'Murder?'

'Accident. Now, what were you going to tell me about Thursday night?'

Alf explained. 'You'll have to tie the dogs up,' he said.

'Of course. But when do we get the rest of the money? I don't want to load up and have you drive off with our precious meat! I mean ... if you did we could hardly go to the police, could we?'

'I know,' Alf nodded. 'So here's what we do. We back the wagon up to the gate.'

'Yes.'

'Dad goes into the house with you. He pays the bill. Mr Pritchard and I load the van.'

'Ye-es.'

'Then Mr Pritchard goes into the house to check the money is paid.'

'And if it isn't?'

'Then he shoots Dad.'

'He'd like that,' the woman said sourly.

In Alf's mind that was the important time. When Mr and Mrs Pritchard were both in the house he would pass the glider up to Sally on the barn roof and fasten the rope to the roof of the van. They would have to hope the bomber's moon didn't shine too bright – or that the Pritchards didn't look up.

Mrs Pritchard turned and walked towards the farm. Tegwyn, eyes on the ground, followed like a dog. One of the women at the street corner spat at him as he walked past. He didn't seem to notice. 'Sorry I can't free you too,' Alf muttered.

He turned and ran towards the hospital. Pilot Officer Ingram had told Alf where to find the workshops. They were in a corner of the hospital gardens, well away from the antiseptic smell. Instead there was the smell of wood and glue, metal and varnish. A cold wind from the mountains carried the workshop smell to Alf as he ran over the damp grass.

Men worked away at lathes and benches making wood and metal objects. Some made furniture and others made brightly painted toys. Most of the men struggled with the tools – many had lost a hand or an eye, others worked from wheelchairs or were propped on crutches. All seemed cheerful enough.

Eric Ingram waved to Alf from the far end of the room and called over the humming and grinding of machinery, 'Here he is!'

The men stopped working and turned to watch Alf as he walked between the benches. Alf blushed. 'Do they all know about this?' he asked the Pilot Officer.

'Oh, yes! Everyone wants to help! They think this is the most exciting thing since they were blown out of the war! Most of them want to sneak out and watch.'

Alf groaned. 'But Dad and me ... we're breaking the law. If anyone finds out, Dad faces a year in jail. I was hoping this would be a bit secret!'

Ingram limped across to the boy. 'All these chaps know is we're helping a young maiden in distress to escape from a fortress. She's a princess and you are a knight in shining armour. It's a fairy tale, really.'

The boy shrugged. 'She's not exactly a princess ... just some skinny kid.'

'That's who we're fighting the war for,' the pilot told him. 'Now, do you want to see the bat-wing in action?'

'Yes please!'

Pilot Officer Ingram called across to a serious young man in heavy-rimmed glasses. 'Is she ready for a test flight, Bill?'

'She is,' the man replied.

The pilot nodded to a large wood and silk fan that sat on top of a bench. 'Take it outside.'

'Me?'

'Of course! You're the one that has to carry it to the barn. You have to get used to it. If it's too heavy and you're too feeble then we have a problem!'

'I carry dead sheep for my Dad in the shop,' Alf reminded him. He waited till Bill folded the wing closed then he picked it up and carried it easily to the door. It was growing dark outside but the moon over the hill was bright enough for him to see the loop where he attached the rope.

'As soon as you open her up the wind will lift her … like a kite. But it's a kite strong enough to lift a girl. So make sure the end of the rope is fastened down before you open it. Otherwise we'll have to send a Spitfire plane to pull you down from the clouds.'

Every man in the hut had come into the cold moonlight to watch. Alf tied his end of the rope around the doorknob of the hut. He tested it. The door knob was safe. Nothing would pull it away.

Then he picked up the bat-wing and walked fifty yards away till the rope went tight. He opened the fan and felt the wind pull the wing up. He held tight.

The wind lifted the wing high above the roof of the hut and lifted Alf with it.

Yes, I know, he should have let go. 'Aha!' you cry. 'That's what I'd have done!' But Alf thought that he could stop the wing from blowing away. He didn't know it was powerful enough to lift him into the air till he tried it. Then it was too late. So I guess you'd have done exactly what poor little Alf did.

Some of the men laughed, others looked worried. 'Haul him down,' Pilot Officer Ingram told them.

Half a dozen men hobbled or wheeled themselves over to the rope around the door handle. A gust of wind, all the way from Ireland, suddenly sped over the mountain top, into the valley where the hospital lay. It tugged the bat-wing higher and the rope strained at the handle on door of the hut.

The handle held firm, just as Alf knew it would.

But the door didn't.

Before the first man could reach the rope to hang on, the door was torn from its frame with a scream of broken hinges. It raced over the grass and into the air.

Alf Turner looked down in shock as the upturned faces of the men grew smaller. 'I always wanted to be a pilot,' he groaned. 'But not like this!'

Brains and a Book

Tuesday 12 November 1940

'Hello, Charles?'

'Yes, Ada. What can I do for you.'

'Where is the boy?'

'The slum boy?'

'Yes.'

'On his way home from school I expect.'

'He should be back by now,' the woman snapped.

'Why are you worried about my slum boy?' the vicar asked. 'You have your own slum girl.

'Because they were seen talking in the school yard every break time. I think they are up to something.'

'Something?'

'Some plan. I came back to the farm this afternoon and the girl had done the milking and mucked out the cow byre. She'd collected the hens' eggs and washed her school dress.'

'Ada, will you get to the point?'

'She had lit the fire to dry the dress … and she was humming to herself.'

'Ada, will you…'

'She was humming *There'll be bluebirds over the white cliffs of Dover*.'

'I still don't see what you are trying to tell me, Ada!' the vicar exploded.

'When she got to the last line the girl burst into song.

She sang the words, Charles. *"There'll be love and laughter And peace ever after. Tomorrow, when the world is free."'*

'Ada, for the last time, what has this to do with me?'

The farmer's wife spoke quickly. 'The girl was happy. She has no right to be happy, the way I work her. She was singing a song about being free ... and she has been seen plotting with that boy of yours. They are up to something and I want to know what. I can keep an eye on her but not on both of them. Now get yourself in that car of yours and find the slum boy. Come up to the farm first. I have the sheep brains you want!' She put the phone down.

It was growing dark outside. The vicar looked towards the purple hills and the moon's glow behind them. And he smiled. 'Brains, eh? That'll be wonderful.'

He gathered his car keys and set off for the kitchen to give his cook her orders.

***

For Alf it was like a dream he sometimes dreamed. He was flying. He was looking down on people below and the moon was soaring above him. It felt as if he would soon be flying around the moon. Even the sheep in the next field stopped to look up at the strange and moonlit shape above them. Some of them ran around in worried circles.

> Sheep are used to clouds and stars, birds and rainbows in the sky, but not boys. They had even seen the odd bit of washing whipped away by the wild Welsh wind. But not a boy. So the sheep looked up. Wouldn't ewe?

The wind chilled Alf's bare knees. He clung tightly to the cross-bar as the wing swung in the wind.

Then the rope jerked and the bat-wing jarred. Far below someone shouted, 'The door has caught in a tree.'

Another voice cried, 'It's our last chance to get him down before he ends up in the North Sea.'

'Here ... hold on to the door ... you chaps ... grab the rope ... now pull!'

Slowly, slowly, the straining men hauled on the line and reeled in the bat-wing and Alf. When he was a few feet above the ground Pilot Officer Ingram grabbed the boy's legs and pulled them to the ground.

The sheep went back to their grazing and soon forgot the frightening sight.

When the wing came in reach someone folded it quickly and the gasping men sank to the ground in relief. 'Nearly lost you there, Alf,' Eric Ingram said.

'It works then,' Alf said and blinked quickly, not quite able to believe what had happened. He was shaking and his teeth were chattering. His stiff lips made it hard for him to speak clearly.

'The thing is it was hard work for us to pull you down on the towrope. We really need that second rope dangling to the ground. It's easier to just pull the girl straight down than struggle against the wind in the kite,' the pilot said.

'So, when the second rope is fastened on it'll be ready to go?'

'No, no! That white parachute stands out like a light in the blackout. We need to paint it black. It's what we call camouflage in the RAF.'

'Can I pick it up on Thursday at ten o'clock in the evening?' the boy asked.

'Well, they try to lock us in at night – especially when there's a full moon and some of the chaps like to go out and howl at it,' Eric Ingram said, rubbing his chin.

'Really?' Alf gasped.

'Oh, yes. They become werewolves – you must have seen them in the horror movies? They sprout hair all over their body and run around on all fours looking for chickens to catch and kill.'

'You're joking!'

'Oh, yes!'

You may remember I told you boys' jokes are different to girls' jokes. Young men's jokes are worst of all.

'You nearly kill me and then you tell jokes?' Alf raged.

'It stopped you shaking,' Pilot Officer Ingram pointed out.

97

And, sure enough, Alf had forgotten his scary experience. It's true his hair was standing on end, but it usually was.

Alf walked back to the hospital gates with Eric Ingram and they agreed the place where they'd meet. As the boy turned and waved, a car rumbled round the corner and skidded to a halt. The window slid down and the Reverend Rees poked his head out. 'Young Arthur?'

'Alf.'

'Why aren't you back at the vicarage? Get in the car. There are fires to be laid before you can have your supper. Mrs Pritchard has given us some sheep brains to cook … seems the sheep was run over by a truck. The foolish driver had blackout masks over his headlights.'

Alf climbed into the passenger seat, moving the parcel off the seat. It was soft and squidgy and wrapped in newspaper. A slice of boiled brain would be nice, he decided.

Boiled brain is very tasty, but don't try human brain. If it is the brain of a Gory Stories reader it will be too big to fit in a pot. If it is the brain of a teacher it will leave you very hungry. Know what I mean?

'So?' the vicar said. 'What were you doing at the hospital?'

'Charity,' Alf said quickly.

'Ahhhh!' the man in the black suit sighed. '*Though I speak with the tongues of men and of angels, and have not*

98

charity, I am become as sounding brass, or a tinkling cymbal.'

'Yes,' Alf said.

'What sort of charity?' the vicar asked suddenly.

'I read ... to the men whose eyes were damaged in the war!' the boy said quickly. And he was ready for the next question.

'What did you read?'

'*Moonfleet* – a story about smugglers,' he said. And as he'd been reading it in class each day he was even ready to tell the vicar what the story was about.

'Ah, *Moonfleet*, yes. I loved that book as a boy.' The headlights lit the hedgerows behind the vicar's head. Alf could see the curved nose and up-turned chin, just like his sister, Mrs Pritchard. The man said cheerfully, 'A story about life on a farm in Scotland in the Middle Ages.'

A trap, waiting for Alf to walk into. 'Sorry, sir, I think you must be mistaking it with another book. *Moonfleet* is about smugglers in England a couple of hundred years ago.'

The vicar nodded. 'Of course, Albert. It's some years since I was at school. Before the Great War, in fact.'

They drove on in silence, turned into the dark drive of the vicarage and up to the door. Alf picked up the bundle of sheep brains. 'I'll take these round to the kitchen for Cook,' he offered.

'Don't forget your book.'

'Which book?'

'*Moonfleet*.'

'Oh ... it wasn't my book, sir. The book was lying around in the hospital.'

The vicar nodded, satisfied and went into the house. He picked up the phone and dialled. 'Ada? The boy doesn't seem to be up to anything!'

'Charles,' his sister groaned. 'You always were the stupid one in the family. Take my word for it. He is up to something with the girl – they are thick as thieves. Miss Goodsir told me in the shop. Keep an eye on him.'

'I'm a busy man, Ada…'

'Busy? Pah! Busy? Nonsense! You drive around the village all day, wasting petrol, visiting all the pretty wives whose husbands are away fighting. You don't visit the old, the sick and the ugly, do you Charles? Eh? No answer? You don't do the sad and miserable work a vicar's expected to do. Well? Do you? Cat got your tongue?'

This is an odd thing to say. Why would a cat want anyone's tongue? Unless you stuck your tongue out at the cat. The cat would then lash out at you with its claws and catch it! Which is a lesson for all of us: never stick your tongue out at a cat. It's amazing what useful lessons you can learn from reading Gory Stories.

The man muttered, 'I'll do my best,' and he put the phone down. 'If it wasn't for the money you bring in, little sister, I would happily do the 'sad and miserable' job of reading your funeral service.'

***

Tommy Turner the butcher stood at the gate to his back yard, enjoying a cigarette while he waited. At last he heard boots clack along the back lane and a wheelbarrow creaking towards him. He sucked on the cigarette till the end glowed.

'Put that light out!' an ancient voice cried, creaky as the wheelbarrow.

The butcher laughed. 'Hello, Murphy. You've brought me petrol then?'

'Ten gallons like I promised.'

'Good man. You'll not believe the bit of steak you'll get when I get back!'

'It'll be well roasted if you don't put that fag out. This petrol can leaks a bit, you know.'

The butcher ground out the cigarette under his boot heel and kicked the sparks till they were dead. He opened the back door of his van and lifted the heavy, five gallon cans aboard. 'See you Thursday,' he promised.

Old Murphy clacked and creaked down the back lane.

A voice in the darkness said, 'What's going on here then?'

'Good evening, Parksy. I thought I smelled a rat around here,' the butcher sneered.

'And I thought I smelled petrol.'

'Probably your hair oil is it?'

'Now listen here, Turner…'

The butcher stepped forward quickly towards the voice. Cloud-shadowed moonlight glinted on the buttons of the ARP warden. 'No, you listen, Parksy … your job is to check for lights. I'm not showing any lights. So keep your nosey Parker nose out of my yard.'

'That is not true, Turner. We are trained to detect gas attacks … and when the bombs fall we're the ones that have to dig you lot out!'

'But it's not like you're the law … it's your friend the LDV Lawson that I have to watch out for! Or what is it they're called now?'

'Home Guard.'

The 'Look, Duck and Vanish' LDV soon had their name changed to the 'Home Guard'. But the people of Britain looked at the ragtag bunch of old men that made up the Home Guard and gave them another new name. A new name that stuck like mud. They called them 'Dad's Army'.

'That's right … here, I heard a good song on the radio the other day. A new George Formby song about Lawson's lot! Have you heard it? I sang it in the pub last night and they loved it…' The butcher began to sing in his tuneful voice…

'I'm guarding the home of the Home Guard,
I'm guarding the Home Guard home.
All night long, steady and strong,
Doing what they told me I can't go wrong.

One night while out on LDV
Some German soldiers I did see.
They ran like Hell ...
But they couldn't catch me!
I'm guarding the Home Guard home.'

He laughed till he coughed. The ARP Warden said quietly. 'Just think yourself lucky Mr Lawson didn't smell petrol or he'd investigate.'

'But you're not Lawson ... you're my old school mate Parksy. And, on Friday morning, you come round to the shop and I'll let you have the freshest lamb chop you ever tasted.'

'If I have the coupons left...'

'Forget the coupons, Parksy! Know what I mean?'

'I ... er ... know what you mean,' the warden said.

'See you Friday, with a lamb chop,' the butcher promised.

But he wouldn't. Oh, dear me no. He wouldn't.

DARKNESS AND DRAINPIPES

Thursday 14 November 1940

'If you are going through Hell then keep going,' Sally said to herself. 'Keep going.'

She finished the milking and carried the bucket across the yard. The girl could see Farmer Pritchard on the hill behind the house. One of Penlan Farm's two huge carthorses was pulling a wagon with low sides. One dog followed him. The other was guarding the gate.

The man was cutting green vegetables and loading them onto the wagon. Mrs Pritchard had said, 'He's getting the mangelwurzels in for the winter.

> This is not as cruel as it sounds. Mangelwurzels ARE grown to feed cattle but people can eat them too. Anyone who has tried them says they taste delicious. I wouldn't know because I've never eaten a mangelwurzel in my life. And I don't plan to start now just to let you know. Sorry, but there is only so much a writer can do. Eating weird vegetables isn't one of them.

The cattle get nice and fat on them … and they'll do to feed you too,' she'd smirked.

Sally knew the farmer's wife was in the shed in the field, skinning the sheep ready for the Coventry butcher.

So the yard was quiet. It was safe to slip into the house.

She went in through the kitchen door. The stove was burning and a kettle sat on top bubbling happily. Sally closed the door quietly, though there was no one near to hear.

She took the kettle and poured some hot water into a bowl then added cold water from a bucket on the floor. If one of the Pritchards saw her coming out of the house she would say she had been washing up. Sally had no excuse to go into the rest of the house. She only ever went through the inner door to serve the farmer in his dining room. She went through it now.

Sally stepped into the passage and found a small door that led into a cupboard under the stairs. She opened it and found her cardboard suitcase. She clicked the catches and looked inside. Her spare clothes and ration book was in there along with another *Girls' Crystal* magazine and gas-mask.

It was growing dark in the house now but Sally took a moment to peer at the comic and managed a small smile. 'Patricia Mulvaney … a girl who was not the sort to be scared by a bull … but I bet she never did what I'm going to do!'

Then Sally pushed open the door to the dining room. It smelled of old leather chairs and Mr Pritchard's sour, sweaty socks. He always kicked off his boots in the kitchen before he came in here to eat and listen to the radio. His damp feet steamed by the fire and left behind the dead-cat smell that mingled with the burned-rope scent of cheap tobacco.

Sally pulled a candle from a candlestick by the window and found a box of matches on the mantelpiece, ready to light the fire that evening or light the farmer's pipe.

They would beat her for 'stealing' the candle and matches but she hoped they wouldn't notice till after she'd flown. She placed the candle and matches in her suitcase and fastened it. Then she headed for the passage and back to the kitchen.

Sally had told Alf about the hardships on the farm, the awful food and the hard work. But she hadn't told him the worst part … her nights in the barn. Back home it was never dark. Even in the blackout, with the curtains open, there was always a faint glow from somewhere to show the shapes of her dressing table, the bedside table, the bedroom fireplace and the pictures on her walls.

But the barn on the farm showed her only perfect blackness, as dark as Peeping Tom's world.

> Let me explain. Coventry's most famous person is Lady Godiva. The legend says she rode through the city naked on horseback to protest against taxes on the poor. The people of the city were told to look away as she rode. One man didn't and was struck blind. He became known as Peeping Tom.

And in the blackness were the rustles and squeaks of creatures hurrying about their business. Outside foxes barked, owls screeched and hunted animals screamed. Sally tried to shut her ears and spent the dark hours talking to Patricia Mulvaney. She hadn't told Alf about the hideous dark. Alf would scoff at a girl who was afraid of the dark.

She'd asked Mrs Pritchard for the candle the first night she was there but the woman had screeched with laughter. 'It's a hay barn you idiot slum-child. Knock a candle over and you'd burn us all to Hell!'

Now Sally had her candle. It would comfort her while she waited to be rescued. It would show her the barn door and its latches so she wouldn't be scrabbling noisily in the dark.

She stepped from the passage, clutched her suitcase and entered the kitchen.

There was a click as the back door into the kitchen opened.

***

Mr Turner hurried the last customer out of the shop. 'Yes, Mrs Wilson, I think you'll find those sausages are the best you've ever tasted.'

'They'd better be better than the ones you sold me last week! There was more bread in the sausage than meat! I didn't know if I should fry them or toast them with marmalade. Shocking!' the bent old woman grumbled.

The butcher placed a hand on her back and pushed her towards the door. 'They were made by my son Alf and he was never very good at mixing the sausage meat!'

This wasn't simply a lie ... it was a double lie. Alf had NOT made those sausages. And, when he DID make sausages they were good. But it's easy to blame someone who isn't there. Top tip: It is even easier to blame someone who is dead. 'Please, sir, the dog ate my homework ... but it choked on the paper and died!'

'You want to sack him then.'

'He was all I had to help me. We all have to make do. There's a war on, you know,' Mr Turner sighed. He turned the door sign to say 'Closed', pulled down the blind and dropped the latch so it locked.

He quickly swept the sawdust off the floor – the sawdust he scattered every morning to soak up the grease and the blood from the day's work. He used a stiff wire brush to scrape the cutting block clean then he used some soapy water to wash the benches and the counter. He'd be too exhausted to get up and work in the shop tomorrow morning. 'Maybe Alf can look after the shop while I have a bit of a lie in,' he thought.

At least the shop was ready to open. The shop was a grubby little, poky hole in a dirty street full of penniless people, but it was his shop and he was proud of it.

The butcher had a last look around in the fading light. Then he hurried through to the back of the shop. 'I've made you a cup of tea,' Ivy Spencer said. She still wore the white dress with the purple and green flowers but it was getting grubby now after a week of wear; it smelled of stale beer and tobacco, but new clothes were hard to come by these days. 'And I've made a flask of tea for you to drink on the journey and a packet of Spam sandwiches. I hope you'll be all right. I wish I was coming with you.'

'Me too, Ivy love, me too. But Alf knows what he's doing. If he says we need the space for the return journey then we do. Of course,' the butcher said with a wink, 'you could always travel in the back with the dead meat!'

'Wouldn't bother me,' the woman shrugged. 'I spent ten years married to Mr Spencer before he died. I'm used to spending time with dead meat. Trying to get that man to talk was like … like trying to get meat out of your sausages!'

'Don't you start,' the man sighed.

I don't want to keep going on about sausages BUT the people who got sausages full of bread were the lucky ones. The UN-lucky ones got a lot of sawdust. That wood taste nice.

'What time will you be back?'

'About dawn I reckon.'

'Give me a bit of bacon and black pudding from your fridge and I'll have some breakfast ready for you,' the woman promised.

'Help yourself,' the man said and nodded towards the large fridge set in the wall of the back shop. He gathered a torch with spare batteries, the flask of tea and the sandwiches and stowed them in a small knapsack. He pulled the thick blackout curtain over the window and switched the light on. He studied the map carefully.

'That's the fiftieth time you've looked at that map,' Mrs Spencer said as she came out of the fridge with a plate of meats.

'No road signs, Ivy,' he explained. 'I have to have a clear picture in my head of where I'm going. If I get lost I can always stop at a pub and ask the way but these village people wouldn't trust me, would they? It's not often you see vans on the road after dark.'

'True,' she agreed and watched as he folded the map and slipped on a heavy overcoat.

He picked up the knapsack, turned out the light and opened the door. The sky was almost dark now and the moon was rising. 'You can use my shelter if there's a raid you know,' he said.

'Thanks, I'm never happy in my cellar with the beer barrels,' she said. 'Mind, it wouldn't be the same in your shelter without you there,' she added quietly.

'Yes… well … better be off,' he said and climbed up into the cab of the van. Mrs Spencer tugged at his sleeve and pulled him back down. She gave him a quick kiss on the cheek and left a faint red lipstick stain there. 'Take care.'

'I'll be all right,' he said. 'It's you and that bomber's moon that's more of a worry,' he said.

'See you in the morning,' she smiled. Her teeth shone in the glow from the moon.

The butcher said softly, 'Put that light out!'

'Don't you be so saucy, Tommy Turner. You're a married man. Be off with you.'

He climbed into the cab, started the engine and reversed out into the back lane. He waved a hand as he watched Ivy Spencer close the back gates behind him.

He passed ARP warden Park who gave him a quick salute in the light of the masked headlamps. Then he was crawling along the streets of the city. He wove between the trams and the bicycles and the crowds of people hurrying home after a day's work.

By the time the last light faded from the sky he was on the open road to Wales.

***

Sally held her breath. Her mind was racing. How would she explain the suitcase? If they searched it how would she explain the candle and the matches? Not even Patricia Mulvaney could get out of this one, she decided. The whole escape plan was ruined. She'd be locked away for the night and Alf would go home to Coventry. She'd be more alone than ever.

The back door swung open. Tegwyn stepped in.

The labourer looked at her with blank eyes. He blocked the doorway and didn't move. 'Do you speak English, Tegwyn?' she asked slowly.

He shook his head.

'But you understand it?'

The man nodded.

'I can't stand it here any longer. I am running away,' she said and pointed at the suitcase.

'Dogs,' he said.

'I know…' she flapped her hands. 'I am going to fly over the top of them!'

He squinted at her as if she were mad or as if he didn't quite understand. 'Later tonight. When my friends come to collect black-market meat. They're bringing me a glider.' She put the suitcase on the kitchen table, stretched out her arms and soared round the room.

The man gave a slow smile. Then he gave a thumbs-up

sign, a sign that meant the same in any language. He stepped aside and let her out into the gloom of the farmyard. She hurried across to the barn and hid her case under the straw by the door.

She stepped outside. The yard was still quiet. She gripped the drainpipe and pulled herself up to the roof. She had practised a dozen times and knew she could do it in the dark. A piece of string would let her pull the suitcase up after her.

Sally climbed down and set off to finish her evening work, gathering dead branches for firewood and hauling buckets of water from the pump in the yard to the kitchen. Then she peeled potatoes for the Pritchards' supper, swept the floor … 'For the last time,' she muttered … ate her poor meal with Tegwyn and went across to the barn.

Now she just had to wait. With the candle, and Patricia Mulvaney for company, she simply had to wait.

***

Alf chopped logs, built up a blazing fire in the Reverend Rees's room and took himself off to bed.

There was a clock on the landing of the old house.

From time to time he peered out at it and watched the minutes pass.

Nine o'clock … nine thirty … nine forty-five and time to leave.

He lowered his suitcase out of his bedroom window on a string then gripped the knotted old ivy plant that grew up the wall. He crunched softly onto the gravel outside the vicar's window.

The man hadn't drawn the curtains – no ARP wardens here. Reverend Rees was half way through a bottle of port wine and too sleepy to hear the boy's footsteps over the crackle of the flames.

Alf crept down the drive and the moonlight lit his way to the road and the hospital.

'Not long now, Sally. The knight in shining armour is riding to your rescue!'

BATTLE AND BRITAIN

14 November 1940

After a while, butcher Tommy Turner's eyes were used to the darkness. The moon burned like melted silver and lit the road ahead. The signposts were gone but he knew the way. These were the roads where his own father had taken him poaching in the foothills of the Welsh mountains.

'The farmers will be glad to be rid of the rabbits,' the old man used to say.

'Are there no rabbits in Coventry, Pa?' young Tommy had asked.

'There used to be in the olden days. In the days of Lady Godiva. They were run over by trams, son. No one wants to eat a rabbit that's squashed by tram wheels.'

I think he has a point there. You wouldn't want to eat a bit of beef battered by a bus, a cow cut up by a combine harvester or a rat run over by a runaway rollerskate, would you?

'So, there were trams in the days of Lady Godiva? Why didn't she ride on a tram instead of a white horse?'

'There was no electric to drive the trams in those days, son.'

'So … they had trams that didn't go?'

'That's right! The passengers had to get out and push them everywhere.'

'Would it not have been easier to walk, Pa?'

'Not on the downhill bits.'

'Ah.'

It had taken young Tommy Turner years to realise his father had been having a joke. He laughed as he remembered. A light caught his eye. It was the reflection of his wing mirror. The sky was ablaze with a dozen stars, each ten times brighter than the moon.

'Parachute flares,' he sighed. The blazing flares that hung in the air and lit the ground and guided bombers to their targets. 'Some poor beggars are getting it tonight. Looks like Birmingham's turn' he muttered. The butcher crunched the van into a lower gear and climbed the hills to the west. From the top of one hill he was able to look back. The ground below the flares was starting to glow red and orange as the bombs fell and started the fires.

The windows of his cab shook faintly. He turned away and drove on into the deep valley where even the moon was dimmed.

***

Alf Turner stood in the gateway of Sant Hospital beside Pilot Officer Ingram. The pilot's watch showed ten o'clock. They looked towards the eastern hills. A red glow was lighting the clear night sky. 'Some poor blighters are getting it tonight,' the man said.

'A bomber's moon,' Alf said.

'Revenge for that attack on Munich last week. We were expecting it.'

From time to time the rumble of bombs echoed like distant thunder and they heard the drone of an aeroplane engine overhead. 'That's a Heinkel,' the pilot explained. 'He's dropped his bombs and he's on his way home.'

'Why don't our Spitfire and Hurricane fighters shoot him down?' Alf asked.

'They have to cover the whole country, Alf. If they are sent to guard Birmingham then Mr Hitler bombs London, if they guard London Mr Hitler tells his air force to bomb Newcastle or Bristol. They can't be everywhere. Tonight it looks like Birmingham's turn.'

'This is what Mr Churchill called the Battle of Britain?' the boy asked.

'He said that in June,' the pilot nodded. 'It was printed in the papers. Some of the lads read it over and over again ... he was talking about you, the ordinary people of Britain, and us. The pilots.'

Then the pilot began to quietly recite what he remembered...

'I expect that the Battle of Britain is about to begin. Upon this battle depends our own British life. The whole fury and might of the enemy must very soon be turned on us now. Hitler knows that he will have to break us in this island or lose the war. If we can stand up to him, all Europe may be free and the life of the world may move forward into broad, sunlit uplands. Let us therefore brace ourselves to our duties. If the British Empire and its Commonwealth last for a thousand years, men will say, "This was their finest hour."'

Alf just nodded and heard the enemy aircraft engine fade. Then there was the sound of another engine. One that he knew. A Ford van, not an enemy plane.

'Dad,' he said.

He stepped out into the roadway and waved a torch at the lorry as it slowed. It was ten minutes past ten.

***

Sally couldn't read. Even with the help of the candle she couldn't keep her mind on Patricia Mulvaney ... a girl who was not the sort to be scared by a bull.

But at least the candlelight seemed to keep the rats away from her loft tonight.

The rough boy, Alf, had said he'd tap on the door as a sign. She would climb to the roof and he'd pass the glider up to her. She would tie her suitcase to the hanging rope then wait for the van to start off. A toot on the horn would be the signal for her to open the bat-wing and hold on to the cross-piece.

'How do I get the suitcase onto the roof?' she asked the candle. 'I can't leave my school clothes behind. I might never get another lot. There's a war on, you know. Here's what I'll do. I'll tie a piece of string to the suitcase and tie the other end to my wrist. I'll climb up to the roof and pull the suitcase after me.'

She smiled, satisfied, once she'd made up her mind. Then she frowned. 'If the suitcase clatters or catches the gutter they'll look up and see me. Best if I put it up there now, ready.'

The girl fastened the string to her wrist and to the suitcase then carried it to the door. She opened it carefully. An oil-lamp burned in the farmhouse but it was quiet. Away to the east the sky shone blood red. Searchlights crossed the sky like spider webs and shells burned up into the sky looking for the raiders.

She climbed the drainpipe easily, the way she had practised. She hauled the suitcase after her and wedged it safely in the gutter. She untied the string and went to climb down till it was time.

Then she heard the faint whine of a vehicle on the road. It seemed to have stopped and be reversing up the lane. The door to the farmhouse opened and two shadows appeared.

Sally froze. The moonlight shone on her bone-white face and she felt sure they would look up and see her. Or they would see the door to her barn loft. Had she closed the door behind her? It creaked a little. The light, icy wind was blowing it shut. But there were other doors around the farmyard moaning and cattle shuffling in their stalls. The dogs at the gate began to bark. No one noticed her swinging door.

It was time. And it was time for her stomach to start churning with fear – fear of being caught, and the beating she would get. Fear of flying and falling. 'If I'm going to die I want to die at home, not in some filthy field of Farmer Pritchard's,' she whispered.

She closed her eyes and heard her mother's comforting voice. 'Don't get your bowels in an uproar, girl!' It worked. Her bowels calmed at once. 'We never give in. Never, never, never!'

Mrs Pritchard called from the doorway. 'Get your shotgun, Pritchard. We can't trust these city slum people. If they look like driving off without paying then shoot them.'

'Shoot them?'

'The well in the bottom field is deep. We'll dump them in there and they'll never be seen again.'

One of the shadows disappeared and came out with a longer shadow in his hand.

Sally knew she wasn't the only one in danger that night.

The couple looked to the smoking eastern sky. 'Some poor devils are getting it tonight,' the farmer said as he loaded his shotgun.

'Serves them right,' the woman sneered. 'It's their war, not ours. So let's go and make some money out of them, shall we?'

It's always the same. No matter how dreadful the disaster, how woeful the war or terrible the tragedy, there is usually someone out there wanting to make money out of it. Usually there are hundreds of someones.

They stepped out of the door and crunched across the weed-choked cobbles of the yard.

The dogs' barking was a constant roar now till Farmer Pritchard called for them to stop. The van engine was turned off.

Silence fell over the dark hills with only the west wind in the thorn bushes making a moan as it had done for a million years.

I've met people like that, have you? If they haven't been moaning a million years it sure seems like it. When they come near, the cry goes out, 'Pass the ear plugs!'

***

Tommy Turner and Alf jumped down from the cab of the van. The butcher stretched and was ready for action.

He turned on a smile as bright as a searchlight beam. 'Mr and Mrs Pritchard? What a real pleasure it is to meet you finally … and to do business with you. My son, Alf, has told me so much about you. But, Mrs Pritchard, he forgot to mention what a beautiful woman you are!'

'What?' Mrs Pritchard blinked then blushed.

'What?' Mr Pritchard growled.

'Yes, Mr Pritchard, you are a lucky man!'

'I am?' he asked.

'Of course you are!' Mrs Pritchard crowed. 'I am always telling him that. But does he listen? No. Well now he'll have to. See, Pritchard? A man from the city says you are a lucky man to have me and he should know. He's from the city!'

'Uh?' Farmer Pritchard grunted. 'The meat's in the top barn. I'll help the boy bring it down,' he offered and tucked the shotgun under his arm. 'Mr Turner can go in the kitchen with Mrs Pritchard and sort out the money.'

They passed through the gate, past the watchful dogs, and over the straw-blown yard to the slaughter shed. The farmer dragged a skinned cow while the boy carried a sheep.

The butcher watched them from the kitchen window as they made two trips. 'These look like fine animals, Mrs Pritchard. The real thing – not the skinny stuff they breed up our way. Real Welsh Black cattle looked after by a real, skilled Welsh farmer … and his lovely wife. They will sell well back home.'

'You can pay us a bit more then,' Mrs Pritchard smiled her rat-smile.

'Ah … of course there's the risk. It's me taking all the risk of getting caught. A fine, a spell in prison! But I'll tell you what … give me your phone number and I'll be back for more in time for the Christmas trade.'

The farmer and the butcher's son threw the meat carcasses onto the sawdust floor of the van and Alf raised the tailgate and pushed the locking pins in place. Then he rolled down a canvas flap to hide the load from spying eyes. 'I'll sit in the cab while Dad settles up with you.'

Mr Pritchards went back to the farmhouse and closed the kitchen door behind him.

It was time for Alf to put Operation Bat-wing into action.

***

Alf stood in the moon-shadows. The dogs were quiet. They knew the farmer had seen him and passed him fit to be there. But if Sally tried to run through the gate to freedom they would tear at her thin body like greyhounds with a racetrack rabbit.

He climbed onto the mudguard by the van door and onto the bonnet. He used a penknife to cut the string that tied the folded bat-wing to the roof. The nose of the glider was tied to a rope and the end of the rope was tied to the frame of the van's canvas roof.

He pulled the wing down and clutched it in his arms. He hurried through the gate.

The dogs gave a low growl deep in their throats. They stepped across the path and barred his way. They would let the boy through, but this strange thing he was carrying would not pass. Alf slowly lowered the glider to the ground. He opened the back of the van, cut the bottom half of a sheep's leg-bone off and held it in front of him. 'Good dogs! Din-dins!'

The moonlight glinted on the slobber that drooled from the mouths of the dogs. They sniffed the meat. As they came closer, Alf lobbed the meat into the ditch at the side of the road and the dogs scrabbled after it.

Alf picked up the glider and ran through the gate.

He hurried up the outside steps that led to the barn loft and tapped on the door, 'Sally?'

'I'm on the roof already!'

'Great,' he whispered. 'Take the glider. Pull it so the rope is tight and no one will see it. When you hear the van blow its horn open the wing. Hold the crossbar and it will lift in the air.'

'I know,' she said. 'I'll fasten my suitcase on to the dangling rope and you can use it to pull me down once we're clear of the lane.'

'Good idea!'

Good idea? Of course YOU are clever. YOU can see why this could be a little bit of a mistake that will lead to disaster. Someone as clever as you can see exactly what will happen. Can't you?

'The airmen will be there to help,' Alf said. 'Better go.'

The door to the farmhouse rattled. Alf sped down the steps and over to the gate and through it before the Pritchards – or the dogs – knew he was there. He climbed, panting, into the van cab.

'Ready for take-off, Pilot Officer Ingram,' he said to the silvery sky.

FIRE AND FOOTBALL

Farmer Pritchard opened the gate and let Tommy Turner out of the yard and into the lane where the loaded van stood ready.

The butcher was smiling and chatting in a cheerful way. 'We'll be back for more. I've got your phone number now.'

Mrs Pritchard said sourly, 'My brother, Reverend Rees, won't be pleased that the boy is going back with you. That's ten shillings a week he'll lose.'

Mr Turner lowered his voice. 'Tell him to just go on claiming the money! Most billets do when the evacuee goes home. Who is going to check up? There's a war on.'

'I suppose so,' the farmer's wife grumbled. 'But we're not losing ours.'

'You will one day. I remember the song we used to sing in the last war...' he said and he sang softly while even the owls and the guard dogs listened.

It's a long road that has no turning,
It's never too late to mend;
The darkest hour is before the dawn
And even this war must end.'

Bomb echoes rumbled over the mountains, a sheep bleated sadly.

'Yes, well, we'll kill to keep our evacuee ... I mean we love her so much ... like our own daughter, don't we, Pritchard?'

The farmer just grunted and shifted the shotgun on his arm.

'And if you ever fancy a night out in Coventry let me know. A good-looking woman like you would be very popular with the lads there, you know,' the butcher went on.

'For goodness sake hurry up, Dad!' Alf moaned softly to himself. 'The longer you wait the more chance there is of them looking up and seeing her.'

Sally felt like the world could see here there in the moonlight. The bat-wing and the ropes were painted black, her school coat was dark navy, but her pencil-thin legs were white as the stars.

At last the butcher climbed into the cab and started the engine. He edged forward. Alf leaned across the cab and pushed the horn twice. 'Just saying goodbye,' he explained.

Sally spread the wing and the wind from the Irish Sea began to lift her even before the van set off. Then the rope tugged at her and she slid down the slate roof of the barn. For a chilling moment she thought she was going to tumble straight to the ground but the rope went tight and jerked her over the edge. The extra speed gave her the lift she needed to sail into the air.

A moment later she was over the gate. The second rope trailed behind her and the little suitcase swung on the end.

What happened next happened so quickly she was never quite able to piece it together. But the swinging suitcase smacked Mrs Pritchard on the back of the head.

Yes, I told you the suitcase on the rope would be a mistake. And I also told you that you'd guess what happened. So now you must feel very clever. Strange, because you don't look it.

The cardboard case didn't hurt, but it gave the woman such a shock she screamed. She twisted to see what had hit her and saw the bat-wing's shadow against the moon.

Mrs Pritchard was cruel and wicked, greedy and vicious ... but she had a mind as sharp as her nose. She saw in a moment what was happening and her ten shillings a week sailing away. She reached up and grabbed at the suitcase to haul the girl down.

Mr Pritchard heard the cry, looked up and all he saw was a monster bat in the sky. He snapped his shotgun closed and flicked off the safety catch.

His wife thought she could pull the girl back to earth but the van was towing her steadily now and the woman's

feet dragged along the stony lane. And the woman was thin as a starving rake so, a moment later, she was lifted into the air. A gust of wind caught the wing and before Mrs Pritchard could let go she was tree-top high. Now it was too late to let go. If she fell now she'd break her legs … if she was lucky. She'd break her neck if she wasn't.

The dogs looked up in wonder to see their mistress flying over their heads. They'd only seen those red flannel knickers flying on the washing line, not flying on the woman's skinny rump.

Mr Pritchard took aim at the flying wing. From the shadows came the shadow of a shadow. A rough hand pushed the elbow of the farmer as he pulled the trigger and fired. Then Tegwyn was gone as silently as he'd appeared.

The barrel flashed, the gun roared and a thousand lead pellets sped towards the wing.

BAM!

But the knock on the elbow made him miss his target. His wife was in the way. Most of the stinging pellets tore through the housecoat, tore through the red flannel knickers and into her bony backside.

If someone fired a hundred darts into your bottom then you would grab at the sore spot and cry out. That's exactly what the farmer's wife did. 'Ohhhh! My backside, you fool!' she cried.

OHHHH! YOU MADE ME LET GO OF THE FLAMING SUITCAAAA...

The woman tumbled from the sky. She would have made a serious hole in the farm field if she hit it. But she didn't. She landed in one of the thick thorn hedges.

It shredded her clothes, her back and her legs and tangled so tight in her hair she couldn't move. If she moved a finger she was in more agony. But we have to leave her there.

It took Mr Pritchard all night and the next morning to snip through the hedge, one twig at a time, and cut the howling woman free. Even when he reached her it took hours to haul her out. Some people are afraid to fly. Mrs. Pritchard never flew again. In fact it was a long time before she could even sit down again. I have to say that makes me very happy.

The van reached the end of the lane and turned into the quiet road. The wing was a little torn by the shotgun blast and dipped towards the ground. Sally still floated in the moonlight and Pilot Officer Ingram and two friends hurried from the shadows to haul on the rope. In no time the suitcase was untied, the towing rope unfastened from the roof and the wing carried back to the hospital.

Alf pulled Sally and her suitcase into the van and slammed the door. 'Quick, Mr Turner, he has a gun,' the girl panted.

The butcher crunched the van into gear and set off into the night. Alf looked out of the window as they passed the airmen and cried, 'Thanks! This was your finest hour.' They waved back, smiled and were gone.

At last the Turners and their rescued girl were able to settle back and relax a little.

'It worked,' Sally muttered. 'It was crazy, but it worked.'

'You had to be very brave to do it,' Alf said.

Sally blushed. 'I won't do it again,' she said. 'From now on I stay at home.'

The van had climbed to the top of the hills above Sant

Valley and Mr Turner stopped. 'If you have a home to go back to,' he said so softly the boy and girl didn't hear him over the rumble of the engine.

They looked to the east where searchlights scarred the sky. Beneath the beams a fire burned fiercely. A fire that sucked in air to feed the flames and lit the land for miles around. They were over sixty miles away but the burning city was bright enough to blot out the bomber's moon.

'Are you sure it's Birmingham, Dad?'

Alf asked.

''Course, son.'

'Hitler's revenge?'

'Hitler's revenge.'

***

Friday 15 November 1941

The rest of the journey passed like a nightmare. When they reached Birmingham, fire engines clanged past them, heading in the same direction as their van. Mr Turner could lie no more. 'It's Coventry. Thank God we were away tonight.'

'My mam and dad aren't,' Sally said and the words choked in her throat. 'Hurry, Mr Turner, hurry.'

But a police car was blocking the road and the officer told them the road was closed to everyone except the fire engines and ambulances. They would have to take the long road to the south.

The sun was struggling to rise through the smoky, soot-filled air.

'The boy and me … we're all right. But the girl has

family in the city. Is there no way you can let her through?'

The policeman looked at her. 'You're Sally Midwell?'

She nodded. The policeman said, 'I'm just about to head back into the city. Come with me and I'll drop you off.'

Alf was puzzled. He didn't know why the girl would be known to the police. He handed her the suitcase and she was gone without even a backward look. The butcher and his son turned south and as the day grew brighter they made their way into the ruined city. It took them another two hours.

It was strangely quiet. Houses smouldered like black skeletons. Dazed people wandered the streets. Gangs of people tore at the warm, wet rubble looking for survivors.

Mr Turner drove carefully around craters in the road. The closer they got to home the worse the destruction was. They stopped at the end of East Street. The cobbles were streaming with water from a burst water main and it carried splintered doors and timbers, furniture and window frames on the flood.

A police officer stopped the van. 'No way through here, sir. The tram rails were twisted by a bomb so they're blocking the road, and they'll take some moving.' He looked down the smoke-fogged street. 'Them APR wardens were going round telling people to turn out their lights! Hah! There was nothing as bright as the moon shining on the tram tracks. They were like a sign saying, 'Bomb me!' Hah!'

'We live here,' the butcher said.

'Not any longer. Go along to the church hall in Berry Street,' the policeman ordered. He was tired and red-eyed from the smoke. 'They'll give you food and somewhere to sleep. They can also check you off as living – nobody will risk their lives searching through the rubble for you.'

'My shop,' the butcher started to ask.

'Sir, will you just go to the church hall, please?'

Mr Turner saw there was no point arguing. They drove there, reported, grabbed a cup of tea and hurried through the torn streets to their home.

There wasn't a lot left of it. Even the massive fridge had been tilted on its side, the house was as hollow as an empty eggshell and the shelter at the bottom of the yard buried under bricks.

Some people were lifting the bricks carefully and passing them along, in a chain, to clear a way to the door. ARP warden Park was at the end of the line.

'We're not in there,' Mr Turner said. 'It's empty.'

The man pointed towards the hole where the Bunch of Flowers had stood. 'They say Ivy Spencer came in here when the raid started. Didn't fancy having the whole of the pub come down on top of her.'

Suddenly someone near the door of the shelter cried, 'Over here!'

The line of workers gathered at the spot. Alf could see little through the crowd. But he could see the stained material. It had once been white. It had a pattern of green and purple flowers.

'I told you not to take her to Wales,' he whispered to his father. 'It's my fault.'

His father wrapped an arm around the boy's shoulders. 'Blame the man who dropped the bomb, son. Blame Mr Hitler that sent him. Or blame Mr Churchill for bombing Munich and bringing this down on us. Blame me for telling her to use our shelter. You can blame a thousand people, son. But don't blame yourself.'

The boy wept.

'Mr Turner?' a voice said. The butcher looked round to see a grim-faced LDV Lawson with a policeman at each shoulder.

'Not now, Lawson,' the butcher said.

'These policemen would like to ask you about some meat they found in the back of your van at the church hall. I told them it was your van.'

The butcher looked at the LDV man bitterly. 'Thanks … Judas.'

'I had to. Anyway … they're arresting you.'

'The boy?'

'He'll be looked after till you come out of prison. Now, are you going with them or do they have to handcuff you?'

***

December 1941

Alf Turner dribbled the shabby, leather football around the rubble. 'It's the great Clarrie Bourton racing through the middle for Coventry City … he beats one man … he beats seven … he raises his right foot … he shoots … and he scores!'

Sally watched him. She still wore the faded blue school dress. 'Can I play football with you?' she asked.

'There's no one else,' he said.

He kicked the ball gently to her. The girl's skinny leg managed to push it back to him. 'Is your dad all right?' she asked.

'Yes. Thanks to you,' he said. 'You never said your dad was an inspector in the police.'

She shrugged. 'You never asked. He hates the black market … but when he heard the way you rescued me from the Pritchards he was so grateful. He had a word with a few people and your dad got off.'

Alf grinned as he juggled the ball on his foot. 'The meat in the back of the van just disappeared.'

'It's a mystery,' Sally said with a serious face.

'But they say the blokes in the police station had the best steaks and lamb chops in Coventry. I bet you got your fair share?'

'Are you saying…?'

'No, I wouldn't dream of it,' he said as he lobbed the ball up in the air and headed it towards the girl who headed it back.

'But Mr and Mrs Pritchard are going to prison for six

months each,' Sally told him.

'And the vicar?'

'No. They couldn't find anything to charge him with. Sorry.'

'Never mind. I'm not going back.'

'Me neither. Coventry's a mess so there's not a lot left for Mr Hitler to bomb. We're as safe here as anywhere.'

'That's true,' the boy said and hit the ball against a new wooden door.

Suddenly the door was torn open and Mrs Sheldon stood there. 'What have I told you about banging that blasted ball against my door? Eh? It's a new door after what them Nazis did to the old one! Now you come along and try to wreck it.'

Sally walked across to her. 'Sorry, Mrs Sheldon. I'll see he doesn't do it again.'

The woman folded her arms and huffed, 'You make sure he doesn't.'

The boy and the girl walked down the lane, over the icy, broken cobbles. 'It'll get better so long as we never give in. Never, never, never. What is it your dad says?'

Alf bounced the ball and recited,

'It's a long road that has no turning,
It's never too late to mend;
The darkest hour is before the dawn
And even this war must end.'

Alf didn't tell her his father often went to the ruined shelter at the bottom of the yard singing that song. He sang softly, *'And even this war must end…'* then added quietly, 'But for some it's already ended.'

EPILOGUE

The first bombing of Coventry was on 25 June 1940 when five bombs fell on the Ansty Aerodrome. This was followed by bombs on the Hillfields area of the city which led to 16 deaths.

On 25 August 1940 another raid killed more and left the city's new cinema, the Rex, ruined.

In October 1940 several smaller raids left 176 dead. There were many victims in Ford's Hospital in Greyfriars Lane. Worse was to come.

On 8 November 1940 the RAF bombed Munich which was the home of the Nazi Party. Hitler swore that 'an attack on the capital of the Nazi movement would be punished.' Hitler wanted revenge.

On the night of 14 November 1940 came the attack on Coventry, code-named *Moonlight Sonata*. Five hundred German bombers flattened the city, dropping 150,000 firebombs and 500 tons of high explosives, as well as 130 parachute mines.

The attack went on for 10 hours, from dusk until dawn. Over 200 fires were started.

By the morning of 15 November 1940, 554 men,

women and children lay dead.

In 1944, British Air Force prisoners planned to escape from their prison camp. They built a glider.

The war ended in 1945 before they could use it. But they reckon it would have worked.

It was a brilliant idea.

War can bring out the worst in people. People who make money from the misery.

War can bring out the best in people. The cleverest ideas, the bravest actions, the most stubborn courage.

Some people find the courage to never give in. Never, never, never.

If you enjoyed Blackout
in the Blitz, then you'll love
five more Gory Stories,
written by Terry Deary.
Why not read the
whole horrible lot?

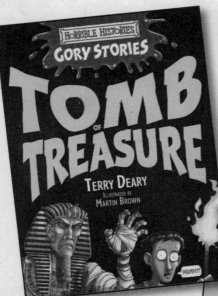

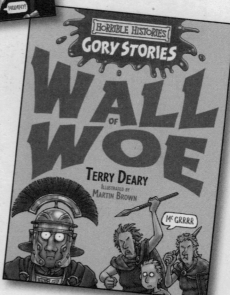

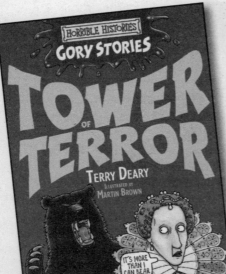

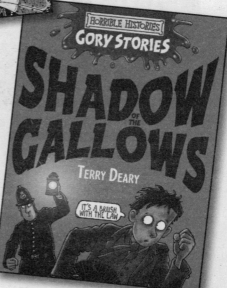

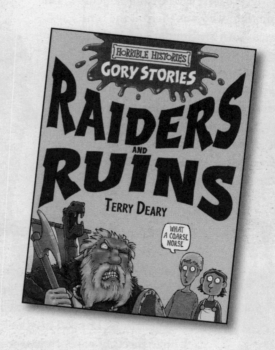

All the GORE and MORE!

Terry Deary was born at a very early age, so long ago he can't remember. But his mother, who was there at the time, says he was born in Sunderland, north-east England, in 1946 – so it's not true that he writes all *Horrible Histories* from memory. At school he was a horrible child only interested in playing football and giving teachers a hard time. His history lessons were so boring and so badly taught, that he learned to loathe the subject. *Horrible Histories* is his revenge.

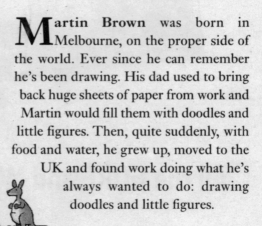

Martin Brown was born in Melbourne, on the proper side of the world. Ever since he can remember he's been drawing. His dad used to bring back huge sheets of paper from work and Martin would fill them with doodles and little figures. Then, quite suddenly, with food and water, he grew up, moved to the UK and found work doing what he's always wanted to do: drawing doodles and little figures.